WALK GENTLY
THIS GOOD EARTH

Also by Margaret Craven

I Heard the Owl Call My Name

WALK GENTLY THIS
GOOD EARTH

MARGARET CRAVEN

G. P. PUTNAM'S SONS, NEW YORK

SBN: 399-12040-8

Library of Congress Cataloging in Publication Data

Craven, Margaret.
  Walk gently this good earth

  I. Title.
PZ4.C8965Am   [PS3553.R277]   813'.5'4   77-22492

PRINTED IN THE UNITED STATES OF AMERICA

For Father and Wilson
And the unforgettable summers
of a far, far western childhood.

CONTENTS

Part One

AM I THE FIRST?

Part Two

AM I THE LAST?

8   *Contents*

Progress and science may perhaps enable untold millions to live and die without a care, without a pang, without an anxiety. They will have a pleasant passage and plenty of brilliant conversation. They will wonder that men ever believed at all in clanging fights and blazing towns and sinking ships and praying hands; and, when they come to the end of their voyage, they will go their way, and the place thereof will know them no more. But it seems unlikely that they will have such knowledge of the great ocean on which they sail, with its storms and wrecks, its currents and icebergs, its huge waves and mighty winds, as those who battled with it for years together in the little craft, which, if they had few other merits, brought them into the presence of time and eternity, their Maker and themselves, and forced them to have some definite view of their relations to them and to each other.

Essays by a Barrister
Fitz-James Stephens
London, 1862

Part One

AM I THE FIRST?

1. Last Summer of Childhood

They slipped through the door into the quiet dark and ran
single file up the needled path to the clearing. The winds had
slid down the peaks in the night. The air was cool and
bracing. Somewhere behind the ranges the morning star
shone brightly in a sky swept clean of cloud. Any instant
now, dawn would step in, shy as a little fawn, bringing that
light which is more precise, more exact, than any blaze of
noon or crimson of sunset.

Seventy yards in front of them and sixty-three hundred
feet above them stood the dark shape of Church Mountain,
one of the minor Cascade peaks, magnificent, massive, totally
solemn. They could see dimly the faint outlines of the great
spruce, the hemlock, the red cedar, the Douglas fir, which
grew on each side of the little forest road where they rode

the cayuse pack ponies as far-western children ride, like young Indians, without mannerism, with utter abandon and with joy.

They knew the place where they could reach from the saddle and touch the mountain's side, the maidenhair fern tumbling down the cliff. Above the cliff they knew where the windflower grew, the wake-robin lily, the bishop's cup. They knew where the branches were so thick no sun, rain or snow ever reached the road, the sun filtering down in an eerie green. And they knew where the road ran like some wild thing along the mad gray-white glacial waters of the Nooksack River and on to the end of this last lovely little valley tucked among the final ranges that led to the great snow mountains of Shuksan and Koma Kulshan.

As the light grew slowly, they could see now the high meadows where the trees stood in small feudal groups, and above the timber line to the steep and burnished rock, to the chimneys that led to the serrated top and the two faint white spots that were all that was left of the winter's snow.

The first year Father had brought them here and they had heard the roar of the small avalanche of the snows in the chimney, they had not known what made it. Last year they had lifted their heads in play a hundred times, and watched and missed it. But this year they were riding the ponies straight toward the mountain on the first warm day of July and saw the snows in the chimney begin to slide, filling the blue sky with a white mist, and they had waited for what seemed an interminable time for the roar that filled their lives with wonder and with awe.

To the right of the clearing, in the dirt road that traversed the settlement, bugs shone brightly from the branches of the firs. These were prospectors' lanterns, made from lard pails by fastening one end of the handle to the bottom of the pail and affixing in the bottom center a short fat candle. Mr. McKenzie, who owned the livery stable, had brought up the pack ponies, the noble steeds of their youth, Rags, Pinto, Birdie, Paint, Nellie and Maude. Father, the lawyer, was there with his friends from the northernmost Puget Sound town—the congressman, the postmaster, the senator and the circuit court judge from Seattle.

The children walked forward slowly. Rags neighed softly, and so did Pinto and Bob. And why not? Each summer the young Westcotts kept them in oats. They rode every day at twenty cents a ride, time unlimited, but no bringing the ponies back lathered and spent. Furthermore, Father insisted they earn the money themselves. How much kindling had Ed and Jim, the twins, chopped in the woodshed? How many cords of wood had Neal, family member by mutual adoption, piled neatly? How many starched petticoats and linens and camisoles had Angela ironed to perfection while Cathy sloshed her way happily through the dinner dishes, the Westcotts' Maria returning to the dishpan every utensil that did not suit her, and reminding Cathy to wipe up the water she inevitably spilled on the floor?

The young Westcotts approached slowly, something almost piteous in their eyes. Father and his friends were hurrying to be off, speaking softly. Through their voices ran a little wind of anticipation, of some deep and inner happiness seldom heard in the voices of grown-ups.

They were almost ready to start. The tents, the sheepherder's stove, the food, the homemade sleeping bags, each rolled with its blankets, were packed. The children watched their father stowing his ice ax, his precious ropes and, lastly, his climbing boots. Each year the hobnails and the calks were carefully replaced. The boots, shining with the hot grease with which he had rubbed them in a rite almost sacrosanct, were then placed upside down on the long alpenstocks to dry.

"In this country, where it can rain every summer and usually does," he had announced laconically, "a mountaineer is no better than his feet."

Now Father had his knee against Nellie's fat side and was tightening the cinch for the last time.

"Come, girl," he said softly, "Give ——," and Nellie noisily let out the air she had been holding so staunchly, that is, she let out two thirds of it, and when Father had tightened the cinch and put on his pack, quietly she let out the last third, giving a small wiggle of content exactly as does a plump dowager happily ensconced in her oldest, most comfortable corset.

Oh, surely Father would turn and see them now! How tall they looked in the summer's new tennis shoes and the bib overalls, a row of porcupine quills up one side of the bib, a row of fish hooks down the other side. How long the legs. How skinny the arms, but hard as saplings. How boldly the knobby wrists emerged at least two inches from last year's best school sweaters. Surely he would say what everybody else said, "Good gracious, how you children have grown! When I return, you and I will plan a trip of our own."

He turned. He saw only his dear children whom he loved

better than life itself. He said, "Hello, chickadees, come to
see your old dad off?" And he said to the judge, "No, no, try
a diamond hitch there." He was exactly like Mr. Valiant-for-
Truth in *Pilgrim's Progress* which he had read aloud the last
rainy winter. Already he had crossed the river, headed for a
new and better land, armed only with his courage and his
scars.

Mr. McKenzie was blowing out the bugs and collecting
them. The cavalcade was about to start. They were not going
this time by the forest road. They were going by an ancient
mining trail at the top end of the settlement on a trip of
exploration, seeking a new way to attack the ramparts that
protected Shuksan and its enormous hanging glaciers. They
were going into country where no one had ever been.

There was no need to put the pack ponies on a lead. They
knew the way. They trailed up the road, past the old wooden
hotel where miners had once stayed, used now as a small
resort. Past the store where the children bought their fish
lines, sinkers, leaders, hooks and the little glass jars of salmon
eggs which always bulged from the right-hand sweater
pocket. They passed the saloon where they were not permitted to enter or loiter, crossed the tracks of the logging
railroad and entered the narrow trail into the deep woods.
Then there occurred a moment of sudden hope.

"I'll take the end, Westcott," said the congressman, and
the children saw that the last pony was Maude, whom they
knew too well. Here the trail led through the thickest part of
the rain forest, intertwined with undergrowth and dead fall.
When the sun was high and the hornets and the horse flies
went to work on Maude, she would back into the thimble

berries, the bracken, the ferns, the alder, the fallen trees. Manfully, the congressman would try to haul her out, whereupon Maude would maneuver him deftly into the devil's club with its sharp spikes, and when they hit his tender nether regions he would drop the reins and yell "ouch," and dear Maude would turn on a penny and bolt down the trail for the stable and the Westcotts' oats, a thought which filled the children with delight. But Father ruined it.

"No, no, I'll bring up the rear," he said. "Now, children, you can tag along a bit if you wish."

The children tagged along until the men ahead began to hit their stride, neither too slow nor too fast, coordinating their breathing with their pace.

"This is far enough," said Father, and he kissed Angela and Cathy, shook hands with Ed and Jim and Neal. "I want every one of you to mind Maria," and in that horrible mellifluous tone used by the old to mitigate a small ache of the young, he added, "and when you get home to the cottage, you may eat all the waffles you want with real maple syrup."

Two years ago this had worked beautifully. The children had raced home to consume an immense number of waffles swimming in butter and drowned in syrup. Last year it had worked slightly less well. This year it wasn't going to work at all. Then he was gone. They heard the last hoofbeat on the soft duff trail. They heard their father cry out, "*Nesika kiatawa sahale,*" which is Indian and means, "Let us go higher." And suddenly the silence was louder than any noise.

If you grow up where a snow mountain lifts its proud

crown on the home horizon, in some strange way it becomes a member of the family.

"Koma Kulsham isn't dead, is it, Daddy?" This was Cathy when seven, and Dad had answered, "Why, sister, of course it isn't dead. It's a volcano and it's asleep. It's taking a nap exactly like Mrs. Beanor in her front-porch hammock across the street. Only, come to think of it, among all the noises a mountain can make, I don't remember snoring as one of them."

"And if we eat all our spinach and drink all our milk, will you show us the crater where the sulphur turns the snow yellow?" This was the unidentical twins, aged five.

"I will show you where the fumes rise from the fires that still burn from the creation of our world."

Yet here they were for the third summer, so close an eagle could soar to the snow mountains in a very short time. Here they were, tucked at the foot of the last ranges, and they hadn't seen a snow mountain yet.

They sat down on a log which edged one side of the narrow trail. There was no danger of a deer breaking cover or a bear rambling across the trail. There were no game trails here. Nothing moved. No one spoke. For the first time in their lives the young Westcotts gave themselves over to that deep meditation which is said to be the beginning of wisdom.

2. The Islands and the Remittance Man

These were the days before affluence, when, by modern standards, most Americans were poor even if they didn't know it. They were also independent, self-reliant, hard-working and possessed of both pride and character. In the small towns of the country, and especially in those of the Far, Far West, a region so remote the East was scarcely aware of its existence, the oldest of American habits held firm. Summer belonged first to children. Wise parents knew well that many of their offspring, and especially the ambitious, would move away to find work, and that all of them, even those who, with great self- and parental help had managed to educate their heads, would start in exactly the same place, down at the bottom at fifteen dollars a week and often less. It was only fair, therefore, to cast one's brood into the lovely summers like fingerlings into the sea, like fledglings into the air, to grow up slowly, to gather embers to warm their hearts when the going grew rough—and the going was bound to grow very rough indeed.

In the northernmost Puget Sound towns close to the border, it was customary to take one's children, when small, to the San Juan Islands and turn them loose. John Westcott did this soon after he arrived from Montana with his four children and Maria, who had been with him since his wife's death. He pitched two tents in the orchard of his friend and client, Mr. Keith-Hutton, a remittance man, who loved the children and adored Maria's cooking. The children played on his little shingle beach. They lay on his float watching starfish and schools of minnows. They caught on bent pins every bullhead in the Sound and threw them back in. This went on for several years.

It was obvious then to Keith-Hutton that Angela, the eldest, was no problem at all, already a perfect little lady and headed for beauty. But that Cathy! She wore the marks of the true tomboy, freckles on her nose and scabs on both knees. Every morning he awoke to a frightful cackle in the hen house, and he knew Cathy was up, happily picking up his brooding hens to see if they were working hard enough.

He acquired at once a distraction, one Mr. Moses, a small mule, accustomed to children and a natural born psychologist.

"Now get on the left side and hold the reins like this," he said, "and off you go."

Mr. Moses moved around the Keith-Hutton acreage at a walk. Cathy, of course, thumped him with her bare heels, broke an alder switch and slapped his sides. Mr. Moses stopped, ducked his head abruptly and pitched her off, spread-eagled on the ground. Then, very deliberately, he stepped up and put one foot on each side of her little spread skirts, and stood. The children hauled on the reins, pulled his tail, pushed and prodded and yelled for help to Mr. Keith-Hutton, who came running. He had no luck, either.

"Well, Cathy," he said, "I think I'll have to lay a little fire under Moses." Cathy giggled.

He got down on his hands and knees, unbuttoned her sweater and her little dress, got hold of her shoulders and hauled her out, clad only in her panties. Mr. Moses was retired from combat.

Two summers later, Mr. Keith-Hutton scored a triumph. He acquired a small, light, metal rowboat called the Scarlet Runner, and taught the children to row. In the long twilights it was one of the sights of Doe Bay to see him, very erect in the aft cross seat, calling orders to his crew like the Ruler of the King's Navee, the children feathering their oars, rowing in a rhythm lovely to behold along the fir-edged shores, the droplets from the blades falling like bright jewels, the fish jumping into golden circles of phosphorescent water.

There were a couple of near casualties, naturally. Twice, Mr. Keith-Hutton looked up from Dryden to see Ed and Jim paddling happily on a drift log out into the current stream, in need of immediate rescue. Also, Maria managed to fall off his narrow pier and had to be resuscitated by the very latest method. He rolled her on a barrel.

The last summer Mr. Keith-Hutton did something which the natives declared could only be attempted by an idiot or a remittance man. He bought water wings and taught the children to swim in water which was forty-eight degrees on a hot summer day. When they could manage without wings, he announced they were all going to dive off the float at the end of the pier and swim to shore.

"I'll go first," he said, looking very knobby-kneed and

genteel in his one-piece bathing suit. Off he went, emerging with a huge involuntary bellow, followed by the young Westcotts, all dog-paddling like mad, emerging on the beach triumphant, blue, and generously covered with goose bumps.

"Having survived this," announced Father, who was there for the weekend, "I believe that next summer I shall introduce my family to their own mountains. That is, Mr. Keith-Hutton, if you will agree to leave your nonlaying hens long enough to visit us and sample Maria's wild blackberry pie."

When Father came the next week to take the family home, he looked a little strange.

"There is something I have to confess," he said. "Your father, with no malice aforethought, has acquired two new family members."

"Male or female?" asked Maria, who was practical.

"Male, fortunately. Our old family doctor in Helena, Montana, was called out one night to an emergency on a ranch some distance from town. He was caught in a blizzard and died of pneumonia five days later. He left me as guardian of his son, Neal Herbert, there being no relatives. He left a small estate invested in an eastern bank for the boy's education. Naturally, I sent for him and put him to board with Miss Graham next door."

"Father," said Cathy firmly. "Miss Graham is a pickle."

"Miss Graham is a commendable woman and a dedicated teacher. She is a model of propriety. She has to be. She has an ancient mother to support. If she marries she will lose her job. I have noticed she is not asked to the ladies' literary societies."

"That's why she is a pickle."

"Cathy, stop that. When I met his train, Neal Herbert was as grimy as a cinder. He's about Angela's age, I think. He was clutching his prize possessions, a very young tomcat, his valise, and in it a tomahawk with five coups for the scalps it had taken. Miss Graham wouldn't let either in the house. Every night when I went home there was that cat waiting at the door, looking half-starved, woebegone, totally forlorn, and over the fence was the boy calling for the cat to come back to him."

"I think I know what's coming," said Maria dryly. "Four days later the cat was sleeping on the foot of your bed, bulging with milk, cleaning himself up and purring."

"I gave the boy the maid's room in the attic, papered with those horrible cabbage roses."

"You were planning to freeze him to death?"

"I had the carpenter put in a small stove that burns planer ends. I also had him make a small swinging panel in the door of the outside back stairs. I moved in a cot and made it up, and a bookcase and chair. When the boy came over to ask, please, would I mind returning his cat, I said, no, not if he'd tack up his tomahawk over his new bed. He moved in last night and I crept up the attic steps in my stocking feet to see how they were doing. It was raining a little, and I must say it was cozy up there with the patter on the roof, and the big cavernous unfinished part of the attic holding my mountain gear."

"Well," said Maria, "how was our new member doing?"

"Asleep and smiling. In the curve of his back was the cat. I must admit he gave me a very smug look. I don't want you to be sorry for the boy because he has known tragedy so young. I want you to remember that his father brought every one of you into this world and helped my Emily die with grace."

Because the roads were so bad, the Westcotts made the trip each year to the last small valley on the much-beloved logging train, one yellow baggage-and-passenger coach attached to the last of the flats. The distance was forty-seven miles, the hazards so varied and so great it was considered wise to take along a picnic lunch and settle down as for a long voyage. The train passed the stump farms where poor farmers were hoping to live long enough to burn, to dig, to dynamite the stumps out of their land. Then it entered the woods. Since it was the only train on the track, it need not dispute the right-of-way with anything larger than a cow, a deer, a horse or a bear. But if the bear was a mother bear with two cubs playing happily in the roadbed, the engineer stopped and tootled his whistle. Mr. Kimble, the conductor, approached the bear. The bear approached Mr. Kimble and chased him clean around the train, the children screaming with delight, the family dogs—they were permitted to sit by the window, naturally—howling. The little train made unexpected stops along the way to toss off medicine for ailing homesteaders, and if a logger was hurt, it rushed him to the nearest medical aid so fast it almost melted the plug in its boiler, the fireman casting wood into the firebox, the big screened barrel stack snorting and puffing. On every trip the engineer was apt to spy a group of Swede loggers waiting beside the track, the tops of their hats cut out to ventilate their hair, their faces wearing that glum look that meant they had announced firmly to the boss, "No snoose, no work." And Mr. Kimble would call out, "Here you are, boys," and toss off a large package of Copenhagen's best snuff. Every summer there was at least one, or two or three forest fires, Mr. Kimble hurrying to wet handkerchiefs for the passengers to tie around their noses. On such occasions, when the train reached the end of the line, he was careful to let the children off first so they could run around the little coach and break all the paint blisters they could reach, one of the attractions of the line.

3. Nesika Kiatawa Sahale

Back on the log in the deep silent woods, after almost an hour's deepest meditation, the young Westcotts had come up with several small nuggets of wisdom.

One, it is not children who can't grow up. It is adults who are absolutely hopeless.

Two, and dear to the heart of every American, independence is taken, not given.

Three (they would not even recognize this one when they collided with William Blake on the paths of learning), "The tigers of wrath are wiser than the horses of instruction." Nevertheless, there was now a very small tiger in the head of each, exactly like the large tiger that hides behind an overhanging rock waiting for the hunter, and woe to him if he doesn't see the tiger's tail sticking up behind, gently waving, its tip curled in joyful anticipation of the pounce.

The young Westcotts knew what they were going to do. They had made a huge leap into the future and landed on the same rock. The trouble was they didn't dare discuss it. Father would be sure to ask, "Which one of you thought up this madness?" To confess was dangerous. To lie was unthinkable. It is possible that God in his mercy could forgive a whopper. Father could not and had no intention of learning.

Cathy stood up. "Nesika Kiatawa Sahale," she cried, "and don't say a word," and the young Westcotts headed for home, like Maude for her oats.

In the cottage Maria was trying to keep the waffles hot and wondering what on earth could have kept the children. Back in Montana Father Westcott, a Protestant, had done the legal work of the Catholic orphanage, free, of course, and upon his wife's death the orphanage had dispatched Maria, a pink-cheeked Alsatian daughter of a Butte miner killed in a slide, to help out with the children and earn her way. She had been permitted to come west with the family on the condition that she be raised in her own faith. Maria was known only in the possessive case. She was the Westcotts' Maria.

When the children dashed in, Cathy spoke for them all.

"Oh, Maria, I have the nicest surprise for you and Father. You know how Father has never been able to teach me to walk a log over a stream. He tells me to keep my eyes on the log and I always end up astride it, with one leg on one side and one leg on the other side, which in a western family is a disgrace. Do you remember those two large logs over the Nooksack to the left of the little road? If Neal tied a rope around me and came right along behind me, I know I could do it. That would bring us out in the lower meadows. It's such a lovely day for a picnic and we will all help you fill out your wild-flower pressing book."

"Why, Cathy, that's a lovely idea. I've been so eager to find some shooting stars."

They were up, clearing the table, doing the dishes. Angela deviled the eggs. Cathy made the sandwiches. The boys filled the canteens. Neal found a stout piece of Father's old mountain rope and a staunch stick. Maria changed into overalls. They were off. It was as easy as that.

The sun was up and shining. The mountain rose above them in all its magnificence, impervious to man and his petty follies. They made their way through the ferns, the bracken, the firs, until they reached the two logs across the Nooksack, left over from the first logging. Neal tied the rope around Cathy's waist.

"Now remember. I'll be right behind. Don't look at the water. Don't look at your feet. Look at the log," and Cathy did it, so pleased with herself she wanted to go back and try it again.

They strolled up through the first meadow.

"Maria, here are some lovely penstemon, and some Scotch bluebells and trillium too."

They crossed the first meadow and entered the second, where the trees stood in small feudal groups. They moved on beyond the timberline.

"Here they are, Maria. Here are your shooting stars."

It was here they had lunch, the settlement already far, far below them. The little marmots that had their burrows on the mountain came out and said, "*Whee-whee,*" and Cathy imitated them, and took off her sweater because the sun was warm.

"Well," said Neal. "Let us see what other flowers we can find for Maria while she is pressing the new ones in her book."

Maria pressed her flowers carefully. How lovely it was to have some time to herself, free of responsibility. Besides, she had a problem that had been bothering her lately. It was not the Westcotts. It was Father Ryan, the local authority for the Catholic Church, who wished to be sure she was being brought up properly, and after mass or confession had questioned her with considerable adroitness.

"Maria, I notice Mr. Westcott does not go to the Protestant Church. Why is that?"

Maria had explained that in the early colonies Father's ancestor and his friend were captaining two crews to build a millrace. To decide which team was to go first, they had spat on a stick and tossed it in the air, and scarcely had it hit the ground before the Presbytery had met and bounced them out of the church for heinous sin and profanation. It had been necessary for the ancestor to move on into western Pennsylvania.

"And then what happened?"

"Well, Father," Maria had told him, "then Mr. Westcott's great-great-great-great-great-grandmother, aged six, went into the house one day to find her beloved Aunt Nan sobbing bitterly because Uncle John had announced that her infant was doomed to damnation forever since the Reverend had not been able to get there in time to baptize it."

"And then, Maria?"

"And then Mr. Westcott's ancestress had said loudly, 'If you don't think a little innocent baby can get to Heaven, how do you think you are going to get there?' It was then necessary for the family to move on into Ohio."

"When will these people ever learn what it means to leave the one true Church? Maria, does he pray?"

"Oh, yes, Father. Almost every night at the dinner table."

"And exactly what does he say?"

He had her. With great fortitude Maria had made a frontal attack.

"Father Ryan, when I first went to the Westcotts in Montana, I was one of the worst liars on this earth. He cured me. He corrected my grammar. He brought me up as carefully as his own children. When the family gathers in the living room to read, he picks my books. I am likely to end up the best-educated girl in the parish. I wait on the table. I cook. I wash the clothes, but I am not a servant. I am a member of the family. I love them and they love me."

Oh, that word *love*! What divine can resist it? Father Ryan had gone down in the flip of a salmon's tail. But with a sigh. "What a nun she would have made."

Maria had pressed the last wild flower. It was suddenly very, very still. She turned and looked toward the mountaintop and saw her young Westcotts at the foot of the burnished rock. For the first time she knew their intent. She knew also her duty. If they were going to fall off a mountain, she was going to fall off with them.

"Come back, come back," she called. Nobody answered.

Maria said three Hail Marys and started after them. She would have said more, but the altitude was beginning to affect her. It was then she was guilty of a thought no Scotch Presbyterian could think if he tried. She would rather go straight to purgatory with her Westcotts than to heaven with anybody else. Poor Father Ryan's gray hair would have turned white. She could feel him snatching her back in the orphanage. She arrived at the burnished rock.

"Now remember what Dad Westcott always says," Neal was saying. "One climber does not follow behind another where a loosened rock might fall on him. I'll go first. The next one will not start until I call to him. If it's too steep, I'll help him with the rope."

They traversed the funnel where the debris from the little avalanche lay. They reached the chimney, agile as monkeys, digging in with toes, knees, elbows and hands, wriggling upward until, one by one, they reached the two patches of snow and lay panting on the top.

Slowly they got to their knees, then to their feet. They saw a sight they could not have imagined, range beyond range of snowy mountains, deep green ravines, a glimmer of sapphire lakes and shining ice.

"Are we the first?" Neal asked. "Did anybody ever stand where we stand now?" And they felt that marvelous exaltation which is so brief.

Cathy ruined it. She walked across the top, lay down flat and looked off the other side—straight down over a mile—and she knew that awful anticlimax that awaits all mountain climbers: "Now that I'm up here, how am I going to get down?"

Neal took command. "It's colder and the wind's blowing. I

think we should start at once. The mist is coming in. It's queer; just a few minutes ago there was not a cloud. We can wriggle down the chimney as we came up, but we must try out every toehold before we put any weight on it. We'll go down facing the mountain. I'll come last. I'll moor the rope to a rock and direct you."

Slowly, painfully, burning their hands on the rope, skinning the fine new bones, they came down. Finally Neal said, "We're past the worst. We're past the rocks above the timber line. We can turn around now."

When they turned, they saw that a cloud was between them and the sun. Around the cloud was an arc with colored bands, and in the middle of the cloud each one could see a giant-sized and misty figure of himself—only of himself.

"It's a miracle," Maria said.

"It's altitude sickness."

"When I wave, my shadow waves. It does just what I do," Cathy said, and they began to laugh, to shout, to play, when suddenly the wind moved the cloud on and the misty huge figures were gone.

They reached the spot where Maria had left her pressing book and the lunch basket, and Cathy had left her sweater. Of the sweater only snippets remained. The marmots had chewed it into fuzz and carried it home to their burrows.

When they reached the cottage, Maria made a fire and put on a huge pot of potato soup, and she sent Neal to the store for sticking plaster, gauze and ointment. The young Westcotts went to bed that night patched like quilts. Only their collar bones had escaped. They were too tired and excited to sleep.

Mr. Keith-Hutton arrived the next day in Father's Model T Ford.

"Had a delightful trip," he said, "only two punctures and one blowout."

When Mr. McKenzie returned with the pack ponies after a day's rest, Keith-Hutton went riding with the children on a little side road that led through what had once been a small mining settlement. He shortened the stirrups. He disdained the pommel. He rode Birdie, who had picked up a bit of single-footing along life's way. He sat very straight, posting elegantly as if he were riding in a London park. They went this time in the long twilight and when they reached the old mine, Keith-Hutton failed to see a wire clothesline, still staunchly strung between its poles. He managed to get two fingers up before the line took him in the neck, and he was knocked flat on the horse, his head hitting the region of the rump with a resounding thump.

"Are you dead?" asked Cathy.

"My feelings are dented." After that he used the pommel and lengthened the stirrups.

The third day of his visit Keith-Hutton hired a horse and a spring wagon from Mr. McKenzie and, with Maria and Angela in the front seat, and Cathy and the boys in the wagon bed, set out to visit a shingle mill, operated by Scotch-Canadian friends, on the road that led into the valley.

"In the days of the first colonists," he told them, "the greatest forest in the world stretched from Canada to the Columbia River. Lightning started a terrible fire. The colonists said the burning trees fell like a bombardment, but you know something? The heartwood of the fallen cedars remained firm and hard. It was from them the first little shingle mills cut their bolts. 'On the debris of your despair, you build your character.' That's Dryden."

"That's Emerson," said Maria.

They stayed almost a week at the shingle mill, the boys housed in the bunkhouse, the girls with the owners. They ate their meals in the cookhouse with the men, which delighted Cathy so much that she announced that when she got home she was going to have pie every morning for breakfast.

"Not if I make it," said Maria.

When Mr. Kirk, the owner, drove his sled over the skid road through the deep woods to the siding where the logging train dumped off his supplies, Cathy and Keith-Hutton took turns sitting beside him dabbing dogfish oil on the skids.

That evening the loggers walked blithely on the belts in the slough.

"See how easy it is, Maria; try it." Maria tried it and the belts slid out from under her, depositing her waist-deep in the slough.

"Maria, look what you've done. You've left a hole in my water," cried Mr. Kirk.

Maria's dress and petticoats spent the night drying around the stove in the cookhouse. Then Keith-Hutton drove his entourage back to the settlement.

The next day Mr. McKenzie went in with the pack ponies to bring out Dad's party. That morning Keith-Hutton departed in the Model T.

"I have one thing to say," he announced at leaving. "If

you find yourselves cast into exile for your mountaineering activities, with nothing to live on but your allowance, come to me and learn from an expert," and he was gone.

The next day was endless. All afternoon the family waited by the trail. Nothing happened. By dusk Maria had Father swallowed up by an avalanche; Angela had him headfirst down a crevasse, and Cathy was close to tears. Even the natives had begun to gather when faint hoofbeats were heard.

Maude emerged first. The circuit court judge from Seattle was leading Maude. The congressman was riding Maude. Father, his face a mixture of greasepaint and whiskers, was doing his best to keep the congressman from falling off Maude.

The party stopped at Mr. McKenzie's livery stable, and all but Father were loaded into his express wagon to be driven to the nearest burg with medical facilities, however small.

"Worst trip I ever had," said Father, walking home to the cottage with his family. "Everything went wrong. It rained. How it rained! The congressman came down with inflammatory rheumatism. We put him into his sleeping bag in the tent and took turns keeping up the fire and covering him with poultices. We didn't even have a chance to break camp and explore around us. Didn't see another human being until McKenzie arrived yesterday. With great difficulty we got the congressman astride Maude, and do you know what she did? Fell off a large log, landed on her back between two trees without a scratch. The congressman grabbed a treetop on the way down and it bent him gently to the ground. Oh, the nerve of these Democrats! He says it will make a splendid slogan in his next election: VOTE FOR THE MAN WHO ALWAYS LANDS ON HIS FEET. He lit on them all right, but he couldn't stand up." When he reached the cottage, Father fell on his bed with his boots on. The children unlaced them and took them off.

"Neal," Father said, "turn the fungi to the wall." The fungi, a product of the rain forest, were as large as pies. Some onetime renter had spent the summer painting them with smiling cherubs, stags' heads, and a thinly clad lady perched in what seemed to be a gooey duck, which is an oversized Pacific Coast clam. This accomplished, Father was asleep in two minutes. Maria covered him with a blanket.

"Oh, Maria," whispered Cathy. "He'll never climb again."

"Nonsense. You don't know a thing about mountaineers, but by this time you should know quite a bit about your father."

They did indeed. On a terrible slide on Table Mountain, Father had saved himself by using his alpenstock as a brake, but in the bosom of his family, let him squash a thumb with a hammer and he was a mere mouse in need of attention—all he could get.

"Neal, set the big washtub in the middle of the kitchen floor. Start a fire and on the stove put every big pan we own filled with water. Angela, you get a sheet and plenty of towels. Ed and Jim, rush to the store and bring the largest bottle of 'Triple H. Horse Liniment—Good for Man or Beast.' It says right on the bottle it can be used for horses, cows, hogs, sheep and men."

All night Maria kept the fire going. In the morning she fed

the young Westcotts first, and when Dad Westcott awoke, she tackled the job at hand. When it was well under control, she summoned the family.

Father was sitting in the washtub, shaved and wrapped in a sheet. He was so tall his knees almost touched his chin.

"A little more water on the right shoulder, if you please, Maria. There—that's better. That is bliss indeed. Now, rub in a little more of that marvelous ointment."

The young Westcotts filed in.

"Well," said Father. "I am feeling much better, thanks to Maria. I have come to the conclusion the trip was not quite as disastrous as I thought. Now I want to hear what you did while I was gone."

Cathy stepped forward, who knew only one approach to life. Collide with it.

"We climbed Church Mountain."

"Indeed! And just which one of you thought up this madness?"

"We did not even discuss it, sir," Neal said. "Cathy wanted to practice walking a log to please you, so we took along a picnic lunch and Maria's wild-flower pressing book, and we went across the Nooksack on those two big logs left in the early cutting. I might say, Cathy did it beautifully."

"And then?"

"Well, sir, we ambled up through the first meadow, helping Maria find new wild flowers. When we reached the second meadow, we found the shooting stars she wanted, and just above the timber line we had lunch."

"And what did you do when you reached the burnished rocks?" asked Father slowly.

"We continued, sir. No, no, sir, not one right after another. We went one at a time past the loose rock, and I went first to help with a piece of your old climbing rope, and we wiggled up the chimney and crawled out on the top."

"And you got to your knees and stood up and you felt that marvelous elation, which is so short, and you said, 'Are we the first to stand here? Are we the first?' And then, with all that exertion, Cathy had to go to the bathroom and not a tree or a big rock in sight. Well, Cathy, what did you do?"

"I wet my overalls."

"It has happened to other mountaineers in mixed company. And then you got the shock of your life. One of you crept to the other side and looked down—straight down more than a mile—and you said, 'Now that we're up here, how are we going to get down?'"

"Yes, sir."

"Well, go on. How did you?"

"It was cold and the wind was blowing. I remember mists were coming in, and a moment before it had been clear."

"Did you come down looking out or toward the mountain?"

"Looking in, sir. One at a time, with the help of the rope. When we reached the bottom of those awful rocks, we turned around."

"In some strange way I am proud of you. It just goes to show that the good Lord tempereth the wind for the shorn lamb."

"But he didn't," said Cathy firmly.

"He didn't what?"

"He didn't 'tempereth the wind for the shorn lamb.' When

we turned, something astounding happened. There was a big misty cloud right in front of us, with bands of light around its edge like a rainbow, and right in the middle each of us could see a giant misty figure of himself. No one else's. Just his own. When I waved, my giant waved, and we whooped and played with them, and then suddenly the wind blew the cloud away and it was gone."

"It was a miracle," said Maria.

"It was altitude sickness," said Neal.

"It was the Spectre of the Brocken," said Father very, very slowly. "It was first observed in 1780 in the mountains of Germany. It's a phenomenon. It usually happens in the afternoon when the sun is low, when the clouds and the refraction of light are just right. It has been seen once on Koma Kulshan."

Father's head rested on his knees. Then he lifted it. Only Maria knew what he was going to do. He was going to shoot one of his ex-Scotch-Presbyterian arrow prayers straight through the left kitchen corner in the direction of the outhouse, a two-seater, the usual catalogue hanging on its nail, a covered walk leading to it, latticed with wild roses.

"Your Honor," said Father in his splendid resonant voice, "Your Honor, I humbly admit I was too stupid to realize how my children have grown. This I shall remedy. But surely, in your mercy you could have saved the Spectre until next summer when I take them to the snow mountains. I have never seen it and I have always hoped to do so. It's enough to turn a man into an atheist."

The young Westcotts would not have been surprised if His Honor had filled the sky with a clap of thunder or hit a tree with a bolt of lightning. His Honor did not even let out a rumble.

Maria motioned them out of the kitchen.

"You know," Cathy whispered to Neal, "I think perhaps we overdid it a little."

That night Maria arose and went to the kitchen door, gazed at the huge dark mountain and made a most solemn vow. "Our Father," said Maria, "I promise you that when I get my Westcotts raised and half civilized, I will take myself to some quiet nunnery and devote my life to good deeds and repentance."

The next week it rained. It did not merely pour and clear up. It rained as only a rain forest can rain, in a slow monotonous persistent drizzle. It was as if a ghostly finger wrote in the gray sky, "Summer is over. Go home."

The Westcotts took the next logging train. They did not look for any paint blisters to break. They rode like young aristocrats who had been shown the land of their inheritance.

Mr. Kimble stopped to talk a moment. "You know that place where you kids ride where the branches are so thick the rain and snow never reach the ground? When the snow comes the deer will remember and return to nibble the grass on the edge, and the cougar will follow the deer. There is no more horrible sound on earth than that of the cougar in the night."

Cathy felt badly about the deer, but Neal comforted her.

"Never mind, Cathy. Just remember what a splendid warm winter the marmots will have sound asleep in the fuzz of your red sweater."

And this was the last summer of childhood.

4. Winter of Content

When the family reached home, Father asked the express-man to deliver the luggage, and stopped at his office to order ice, groceries and the newspapers. Since all were delivered by horse-drawn vehicles, which would take some time, the family walked home.

It was a gray afternoon, presaging rain. When the first settlers had arrived, there had been no land, nothing but water and trees. The first streets had been built, therefore, over the beaches. Old Town, which connected the newer business sections with the residential district where the Westcotts lived, was built over the beach, the water, and when the tide was out, the tide flats.

There were some stores on each side of the street. An oriental shop displayed bottles of ancient octopuses and pickled ducks, plus phials of herbs recommended for impo-tency, which Father did not explain and none dared to ask him about.

There were saloons and cafes frequented by sailors and loggers. Cathy had recommended to Father one obvious advantage of moving to Old Town. The cafe owner never need carry out the garbage. He opened a kitchen window, tossed out a pail of potato peels and down swooped the gulls with much screeching and wheeling.

When the Westcotts climbed the hill and reached their nice big old wooden house with a view clear down the Sound to the Olympics, Cathy said, "Well, it's home, even if it does need paint." This was true of all the town. It looked older than it was, no paint having been invented as yet to withstand the abundant rain and the salt air. On the front porch waited Tim, Neal's cat.

He did not greet them. He raised his tail and stalked majestically to the back porch, which was unscreened, and he sequestered himself under the icebox. The family followed him.

"He's mad at us," said Neal. "He's furious."

Angela got down on her hands and knees.

"Come, sweet pussy," she said in her dulcet tones. "Come to Angela." She was rewarded with a hiss.

Cathy was next. "Tim," said Cathy casually. "We only left you home because we were afraid you would tangle with a porcupine. It was for your own good." Silence!

Neal was third. "Now listen to me, Tim," he said sternly. "You come right out of there. Do you hear me?" And he reached in and grabbed Tim, unfortunately by the tail, and was rewarded for the first time in a long and intimate acquaintance with a bite.

It was now Father's turn. He got down on his hands and

knees. "Timothy," said Father most cordially, "the trouble with you, my friend, is that you do not know you are a cat. You think you are a person. I, John Westcott, hereby certify that you are a better person than many I have known. Come out, sir, and rejoin your peers." Timothy came out.

When the luggage and supplies had been delivered and put away, and Maria was busy with dinner, the family settled into the house as if from a long, long absence. It was drizzling now and on such nights the little towns of the Far, Far West grew close unto themselves with a charm all their own. Along the nice street the children came skipping home from play in their slickers and sou'westers, and when they ran up the steps and opened the door, out floated the tantalizing aroma of home-baked bread fresh from the oven, a flash of lamplight, and always a woman's voice calling the watchword of the land, "Don't forget to wipe your feet, darling."

No children came home then to an empty house. Mother was there, or a grandparent or two, to tie the children to their heritage. No family gobbled dinner and dashed off in all directions. There were very few places to go. No mother need tell her girl child, "Never, never speak to a stranger." An Indian might go to sleep on the front lawn and have to be escorted back to the reservation. Two loggers in from the deep woods with money jingling in their pockets might get into a splendid fistfight that necessitated a night in the pokey. A hobo might help himself to the morning cream from the icebox on the open back porch, but if he did, he was careful to leave the pan within easy reach. Any man, however rough, knew a lady when he saw one and watched his words and his manners.

In the long dusk the cinder burners glowed in the sky. The boats slipped into the quiet bay as silently as if in a dream, a tug pulling a crib of logs, a freighter dropping anchor to await a berth, small fishing craft coming in from Eliza Island or from Orcas, instantly recognized by the wake they left behind them.

It was true that no tugs pulled in huge red scows piled high with silver salmon from fish traps. Years before, David Starr Jordan from Stanford had announced that unless fishing regulations were put in at once, the great runs would cease and not return for many years, and he was right, but no one listened. The world's largest canneries still ran. Fleets of ships went yearly to Alaskan waters and brought the catch home carefully iced.

The Westcotts looked at the gifts friends and neighbor boys who worked on the ships in the summer had brought them. The napkin rings Maria was placing on the dining-room table were made of walrus tusks, as was the fine cribbage board with its etching of seals and dogsleds. On the mantel stood Cathy's small ivory rabbits, beautifully carved by the Eskimo. Under one window was the large Chinese camphor-wood chest, covered with red pigskin and studded with brass, which one of Father's friends had picked up for a few dollars at Sitka, a relic of the days before the Alaskan purchase when Russian officers used the chests as footlockers. And in front of the fireplace was the white polar bear rug, a horror to Maria, who had to keep it from yellowing. It was backed by heavy red felt which extended beyond the fur, only its head stuffed and fierce, its mouth open, its eyes red in the firelight.

Quite often on the cold nights Tim, the cat who had become a person, used the polar bear's head as a footstool, reaching down now and then to give the bear a pat as if he were saying, "Never mind, we can't all be as smart as cats."

Down one side of the living room, which was forty by forty feet were their friends, Father's books, hundreds and hundreds of them. The children had snooped into them all, reading the conversations first, and reserving all long descriptions for the future.

This evening, because it was the first one home, Maria and Angela made fudge. Cathy wound up the old Victrola and played the Italian Street Song so many times Father told her if she didn't stop he'd be forced to put his foot through it. Neal took the twins at Authors. Father smoked his pipe and read.

The next week school started and so did music lessons. The day began for parents of intermediate pupils promptly at six with a strident mixture up and down the street of squeaks, toots and squawks. One hour's practice was required, a half an hour before breakfast, a half an hour after school. Cathy never missed. She attacked the scales which she detested. She raced through Bach's Two-Part Inventions which she despised. Upstairs, her father, who knew what was coming, put the pillow over his head. Cathy was now ready for the new piece.

This time the new piece was McDowell's "Scotch Poem" (after Heine):

Far on Scotland's craggy shore
 An old gray castle stands,

. . . .

And from a rugged casement
 There peers a lovely face

 . . . white with woe
And sings a mournful strain. [etc., etc. etc.]

This was to be played Tempestoso and the instant he heard it, Timothy knew that when Cathy got to the place where the fierce North Sea went into a rampage, she was sunk without his help. Home he raced, taking his place beside her, ready and more than able. And when the music said "f-f-f——risoluto——brioso——f-f-f" and all hell broke loose, Timothy lifted his head and yowled Cathy home.

This, of course, delighted Ed and Jim. Every time a caller came Cathy was asked to play McDowell's "Scotch Poem" so the visitors could hear Timothy howl. Angela played "A La Bien Aimée"—moderato and cantabile—but in this, Tim was totally uninterested.

There were a few very rich families in the town—in resources, of course, timber or Alaskan fish. But they had arrived as everybody else had arrived, with nothing. They had prospered and still ran their empires on the old paternal system. If a farmer well known for his honesty needed a bank loan, he was given it. No mill worker with some crisis at home had to go to his boss to ask help. His boss went to him.

There was a fat turkey at Christmas for every employee and in boom years even a small bonus, and if the mill owner did not pay what could be called a plump wage, who did? Who indeed?

There was also the Lawrence family, said to be worth thirteen million culled in the days of the gold and silver booms in Montana, who had come to the little Puget Sound town when it had anticipated happily being the western terminal for the transcontinental railroad. Mr. Lawrence had built a large hotel in anticipation of the boom. But the terminal went elsewhere and the Lawrence family went to live in the big empty hotel.

When Cathy was little and asked to spend the night with Mary Lawrence, Mr. Ben, their manservant, came for her. When she and Mary were ready for bed in their flannel nighties, robes and bunny slippers, he escorted them upstairs into the shadowy empty depths.

"Now pick out any room you want. I'll make up the beds." With much excitement they made their choice. The beds were made up. Mr. Ben tucked them in.

"I'll leave a gas jet burning in the hall. If you hear a queer sound, it's only an old owl that nests in the chimney, or a mouse bottled up in the grate." He departed, two delighted little girls squealing with pretend horror between giggles.

When the children were older, to be asked to a party at the Lawrence hotel was like being suspended between heaven and hell. The huge foyer had marble floors, and Mr. Lawrence, having thoughtfully provided every vehicle that had wheels and could go like lightning, quietly took himself to Portland and shut himself up in the old Portland hotel until the furor was over. For the children this was paradise. For their parents it was a place somewhat lower down. When it came time for Mr. Ben to deliver the guests back home, many a mother peeked from behind the lace curtains to see if her child was the one brought home by Dr. Riggs, no doubt in bandages and sometimes in splints.

When the rain stopped and the skies suddenly cleared, Father surveyed his day.

"You can see Koma Kulshan," he would announce, "and the Olympics. You can see the Selkirks in Canada."

In Canada along the beaches of Vancouver Island and in southern sections of British Columbia, the Canadians would say, "Look at Mt. Baker (the Canadian name for Koma Kulshan). It is so close you feel you can reach out and touch it."

Thus on every fine day each country saluted the mountains of its neighbor.

It was on such a Sunday that Father and the boys descended the bank from their house to spend a splendid early morning shooting at hell-divers. At Sunday dinner Father was carving the roast when he glanced through the window and saw Mrs. Beanor approaching rapidly.

He shot an arrow prayer into the left-hand corner of the ceiling. "Your Honor," he said, "here she comes with fire in her eye. Since it is obviously too late to run, I ask that in your mercy you keep me a gentleman. Maria, answer the door and ask Mrs. Beanor to join us at dinner. Angela, set another place. Cathy, one giggle out of you and you will be asked to eat your dinner in the kitchen."

Mrs. Beanor was ushered in and seated.

"And to what," asked Father, "do we owe this unexpected surprise?"

"Oh, Mr. Westcott. At six this morning four tramps were on the beach, shooting at those helpless little ducks."

"An outrage. Neal, finish carving the roast while I call the sheriff."

He went to the telephone, lifted the receiver.

"The sheriff, please," he said to the operator. "This is John Westcott speaking. Tell him it is an emergency."

There was a deep silence.

"Sheriff Pound? Mrs. Beanor, our neighbor, is dining with us and tells me that at six this morning four tramps were shooting those fish-eating, inedible, helpless little hell-divers on the beach near her house. On the Sabbath, mind you, a day of peace."

"Mr. Westcott," said the sheriff, "assure the old pest it will not happen again, and the next time try farther up the beach toward Marietta."

"Thank you, sir."

The next week Mrs. Beanor was again pestiferous, and this time she hit where it hurt. There was the family in the living room, homework done, happily reading, when Father let out a mighty roar.

"Who has been cutting pieces out of my magazines?"

"Mrs. Beanor," said Maria, "She cut out all the bits she thought I should not read."

"I shall march over there and lift her forelock."

"It won't be necessary," said Maria quietly. "I went down to the library and read in all the holes. I copied them and here they are. Each is marked with the name of the magazine and the page number."

"Maria," said Father, "you have averted a calamity. You are the Westcotts' jewel."

American history at school was not a matter of dull facts and dates. It was filled with little bits of family history contributed by every child.

"My grandparents escaped from Germany in a load of hay because they were sick of wars and tired of being pushed into the gutters when the Junkers walked by."

"My Norwegian great-grandfather was caught in the Russian revolution. He fashioned a pair of skates from barrel staves and he skated down the Neva and reached Harbin and came here on a fishing boat."

"In the town where my family lived in south China there was a year of flood and famine. One day my father saw an old man fall off a bridge. He was so close to the bridge that anyone on that side could reach out a hand and save him, but nobody did because he was just one more mouth to feed. My father made up his mind he would reach America no matter how long it took him, and he did."

Keith-Hutton arrived three days before Christmas, and the family, with the exception of Maria, walked to the edge of town, where the forest began, to choose the tree. Neal took his tomahawk to cut it down, a stout small ax traded by the Hudson's Bay Company for furs and used by the Sioux to cut off the fingers of their victims to get their rings as well as their scalps.

Father was very particular about the tree. It must be a Douglas fir. Enough snow must have rested on its boughs to level the branches sufficiently to hold upright the candles. It was found and cut, whereupon Tim tangled with a skunk. Neal had to run all the way home so Tim could be held on the running board, dunked in four tubs of water, soaped, rubbed in four old Turkish towels, sprinkled with Father's best bay rum and returned to the head of the polar bear, sneezing but totally unrepentant.

Christmas Eve the family trimmed the tree, and when the lights were out, one by one they sneaked down with their simple presents. Christmas breakfast, of course, was interminable. Father pressed second helpings on everyone. Then came the great moment. Father went into the living room by himself and lighted the candles and one by one they slipped into their seats, squinting their eyes to heighten the magic of the lights.

There were the usual new books and records, the *Youth's Companion* and *St. Nicholas,* the needed sweaters and pajamas. Then Father said, "I believe, Neal, if you open the door to the cloak closet you will find Keith-Hutton's, Maria's and my contributions for the summer's trip to the Snow Mountain."

There were sleeping bags made by Maria, each rolled with its blankets provided by Father. For each young Westcott there was an alpenstock from Keith-Hutton, its height measured for the individual, its pike bright, its shaft splinterless, its rawhide strong. There was an envelope from Father which read that he would be pleased to provide the heavy jackets, the wool socks, and the hiking boots and assist each to put in his own hobnails and to apply the oil.

While Keith-Hutton was with them, there occurred one of the town's greatest joys. A first-rate stage production played a one-night stand on its way from Seattle to Vancouver. Each year this happened two or three times. They had seen *The Blue Bird*. They had seen Maude Adams in *The Little Minister*. They had seen Pavlova and so close Cathy spotted the vaccination mark on her arm and felt an immortal bond between them. They had seen Kreisler amble out holding his violin like a goose by the neck. This year it was *Little Women*, and Angela sniffed delicately, but Cathy cried so hard when Beth died Keith-Hutton insisted she had raised the sound level at least two inches. And they had filed out into the night, hoping nobody would say a word and break the spell.

Then Christmas was over. Every day Cathy marked off the day from the calendar. Slowly, slowly, through the drizzle, beyond the shining snowy mountains on the clear cold days, summer was coming.

Quite often Cathy would go up into the attic to look at the new sleeping bags to be sure the mothballs Maria had tucked among the new blankets were working, to rub her hand over the new alpenstock which was to be hers. One day while she was thus happily engaged, Tim sniffed from behind a rafter a subject considered so taboo it was unspeakable. Tim unearthed sex.

Mothers then did not discuss the birds and the bees. Neither did fathers. They bought a series of small red books, tucked the proper book for the proper age into the library, knowing it would be found and read. The books were:

What Every Young Girl Should Know, What Every Young Boy Should Know, What Every Young Woman Should

Know, What Every Young Man Should Know, What Every Young Wife Should Know, What Every Young Husband Should Know.

Father had long since tucked in the first and second books. He had hidden the remainder behind the rafters.

Cathy sat right down and read every one of them. Then she called Neal, who read them also.

"Well," said Cathy. "They are the dumbest books I have ever read. It does say that there are certain times when a young woman should not get her feet wet, and when a young husband should be unusually kind and considerate. I suppose that's something. Do you know what I'm going to do? I'm going to ask Father."

"Cathy, you wouldn't dare."

"Yes, I would. What I need is a reason, some way to lead into it. We'll look in all the old trunks."

They looked in the old trunks full of relics brought from Montana and it was Neal who came up with the needed object. He held it up. They could scarcely believe it. It had a French label. It seemed to be a pair of very full accordion-pleated chiffon- and lace-trimmed panties.

"Whatever it is, it's exactly right. I'll drape it over the foot of the bed, and when Dad comes up to tell me good night, as he always does, he's bound to see it and say something."

Dad's nightly visits were often educational. Only last week when he came to see what kind of a day Cathy had had, she had poured out a torrent of invective against her best friend, who had babbled a secret.

"I'm never going to have another close friend. I'm not going to love anybody. To love is to suffer," and Father had stood up gravely and answered, "Cathy, I must admit you are right. You are absolutely right. To love is to suffer, but it is to live much more, too. Good night, my dear."

This night she could hardly wait. She lay there in her brass bed with the light on, the panties spread in full view. At last in came Father. He picked them up slowly.

"I remember them well. When Emily and I first went to Montana, we took a violin, a roll of carpet, and a most somber but excellent etching. We thought we were going to a wild and savage land. Instead, it was a time of boom and Helena turned out to be the richest city in the world per capita. It bought more fine wines, more oriental rugs and caviar than any place in the country except New York. Some of the ladies of the town had their gowns made in Paris. When we had been married some years, Emily bought the panties. She went into the kitchen—we had Nora then—picked up the lacy sides, whirled around and said, 'Nora, how do you like them?' and just then a hobo looked in the back door and went out and collapsed on the fence in laughter. So of course she had to try them on me."

"And did she?"

"She did. That night, when I went to go to bed, she held up the full sides like a ballet skirt and whirled around, and she said, 'John, how do you like them?' and I said, 'Cover a figure like yours with a thing like that?' and I scooped her under one arm, stripped them off, rolled them into a ball and tossed them to the top shelf of the closet, and I said, 'There, that's where they belong.'"

"And then?" said Cathy very slowly.

"And then we laughed. That night, for the first time, we

discovered that sex between two people who love each other can be warm and glowing and lovely. I can't imagine life without it."

"Dad, Tim found all the little red books, and Neal and I read them."

"Never mind, dear. Dr. Riggs and I have considered the matter. We have no intention of sending our daughters out into this world as dumb as violets. There's a new book out. When you are all in high school, Dr. Riggs is going to put it in the cover of *The Little Shepherd of Kingdom Come* and ask his daughter to circulate it among her friends. Fifty years from now it would not lift an eyebrow in the most prudish head. Today it would put Mrs. Beanor into a dead faint. If I were you, I would not mention this matter except to Neal."

"Father."

"Yes, Cathy."

"Thank you."

One day Father met the Reverend McCarthy of the Presbyterian Church on the street.

"John," said the Reverend, "when are you returning to the church of your ancestors?"

"Well," said Father thoughtfully, "let me ask you something. Do you still discuss whether hardwood or softwood is burned in hell?"

"John Westcott, you know perfectly well that it has been years since we wasted time on such trivia."

"Yes, I do. I have noticed also that no school dance has ever been permitted in the high-school gym. The class that gives a junior or senior prom has to hire a hall, which raises the prices of the tickets so high many cannot attend."

"It's the Methodists," said the Reverend McCarthy, very red in the face. "I assure you I tried."

"You work on the Methodists. I'll work on you. It's possible we may all learn the Almighty is larger than we think. Good day, sir."

Mrs. Beanor was over the next Sunday just in time to be asked to dinner, with news which made her face beam.

"My aunt and uncle are coming for a visit from Philadelphia, and I hope you will permit me to bring them to call. They have never been west. I fear, Mr. Westcott, you may find them just a trifle provincial. They have always said they were glad it has never been necessary for them to know anyone born west of Pittsburgh."

"Mrs. Beanor, I am delighted. We shall ask them to dinner. It will be a pleasure to meet them. I anticipate it."

When the relatives arrived, Cathy peeked out the window and announced they were so mild-looking you expected their noses to twitch. They were hereafter known as Mr. and Mrs. Peter Rabbit.

Father set the date for dinner.

"Bring out the Haviland, Maria," he ordered, "and with the coffee, the old silver teaspoons that date back long before the Civil War. And don't forget the Wedgewood cups."

The dinner was splendid. When it was over, the family removed to the living room for a little civilized conversation.

"Tell me, Mr. Westcott," asked Peter Rabbit, "Do you still have trouble with the Indians?"

"Do we? You can't imagine it. Will you believe it, sir, the Lummi Indians have a potlatch each year and each time, until I put a stop to it, asked the white men to participate in a tug-of-war. Naturally, we chose our strongest men, of which I had the honor to be one. The next year we went into the woods and picked the largest loggers. It didn't make a bit of difference. Every time the Indians won. They not only won, but they had an uncanny ability to land the white men on the seat of their trousers in a mud puddle."

"What did you do?"

"I had my friend in the Fish and Game Department send to California for a sack of large abalones, highly prized by the Indians in the making of their artifacts. We have abalones, but they are much smaller. Then I took the sack to the reservation and presented it to the chief and asked if he would kindly refrain from landing us on the seat of our pants and especially in mud puddles."

"What did he say?"

"He said 'thank you' and grinned. We have been friends ever since."

"But Mr. Westcott, don't you regret having no real history? No Trenton? No Brandywine? No Valley Forge?"

"My ancestors fought in all of them," said Father slowly, "and furthermore, we had one really splendid border dispute on San Juan Island. It lasted twelve years. The British lined up on one side; the Americans lined up on the other. Best war that was ever fought. Not a shot was fired, though I do believe there were two fatalities, both dead of boredom. The matter was finally arbitrated by Emperor William. It involved, sir, a boar and is known to this day as the Non-War of the Pig."

"Did you say *pig?*"

"I did. Then there was the time a tribe from the north shot a white man by mistake and the Navy sent out a small vessel commanded by a young lieutenant who couldn't tell one Indian from another and who shot seventeen innocent Lummi in the greatest anger. Only recently the tribe was recompensed for this atrocity."

Father sighed heavily. "What a summer! I shall never forget it. There we were in our hammocks in the long twilight, our Model T Fords propped up in the alley, usually on an apple box, waiting for somebody to patch a tire, and there were the Lummi driving by majestically in their new Overlands and Buicks. I tell you, it took character."

The Peter Rabbits decided they must leave. When they left town the tide was out, the tide flats at their most odoriferous best or worst, depending upon your point of view.

"Your Honor," said Father humbly. "I am ashamed to say I enjoyed every bit of it. I only regret I forgot to tell them about seeing the family cow riding in an Indian's canoe. Do your best to make me repent." It was the next day that the Peter Rabbits went home, badly befuddled.

Spring came suddenly that year with a terrific chinook, the warm rain that melts the snows. In the middle of the night Father's voice boomed through the house.

"Get up—get up. Come to my bedroom windows and hurry."

The family assembled, including Timothy, of course. There in his nightshirt waited Father, and directly in front of them on the tide flats below the bank was a four-masted lumber schooner grounded in the storm and sending up red distress signals.

In the morning the family was up as soon as it was light, in slickers and sou'westers, hanging over the bank to see what had happened. The tide was in now, the schooner listing like some lovely crippled bird, the tugs already at work, pulling her off.

"Look at it well," Father said. "It is the end of an era." Later, much later, the young Westcotts remembered that night and morning. It seemed to them that it was then the change really began which was to end their innocence and that of the country they loved.

5. The Snow Mountain

When the crocus popped through the earth, the grass greened, the lilac came into bud, Father took his family on Sunday walks, each time increasing the pace and the distance until they swung along with that wiry grace lovely to behold. Then came the glorious day when he had convinced himself they would have not outgrown the boots before the bill arrived. Downtown they went to purchase them, and how particular he was. He pinched their toes to be sure there was room enough but not too much. They must be tried on over the wool socks they would wear. The rawhide lacings must be strong. And the next Sunday he took them up Sehome Hill and introduced them to the use of the rope and the alpenstock. Nothing fancy. Merely the rudiments of the amateur.

"Are we going to the top of Koma Kulshan?" Cathy asked.

"We are not."

Father helped them put the calks in their boots, but he let

each oil his own, Maria heating up a horrible mixture which, she insisted, judging from the smell, could be concocted of nothing but dogfish, goose and bear grease. When the boots were drying atop the alpenstocks in the back yard, the family actually knew for the first time they were going to the Snow Mountain.

Even Tim knew it. When the gear in the attic was sorted and readied, the trunks opened, the blankets aired, he perched himself atop and emerged only for meals.

Each day had its exciting anticipation. Keith-Hutton was going with them. The highest mountain in the British Isles was a mere forty-three hundred feet, Father said smugly. It was high time their friend dangled his feet off a peak so that he could stand living at sea level. The postmaster, Father's old friend, the leading surgeon of the town, the circuit court judge from Seattle, were coming also, and the janitor where Father had his office had begged to come as camp cook, a suggestion which hurt Maria's pride. She immediately demoted him to water carrier, wood bearer and chief pot scrubber. This time overalls might not be warm enough. They must add wool pants and heavy jackets for the colder altitudes. A great mountain, Father said, must be approached carefully and cautiously. It treated all men alike. The climber must know when the snows were firm but not slippery, able to bear the weight of a party without danger of avalanche or the collapse of a snow bridge across a crevasse.

"We shall go high enough for you to know where the arctic zone begins. We shall go where no one has climbed and see sights no man has seen."

There were no maps except one Father had drawn from the magazine put out by a mountaineering club to which he belonged. Only the larger ranges and the largest mountains had names.

This year the young Westcotts did not see their own personal avalanche on Church Mountain. It had already happened. With their gear they went first to the village, in the little coach hitched to the logging train. When Mr. McKenzie brought their gear to the cottage, who should crawl out but Timothy, who had hidden himself carefully in the box of sleeping bags.

"We are going to be a part of it," Neal said. "We are going to share that hushed strange expectancy that keeps all the voices so soft and muted. We are going to be like Mr. Valiant-for-Truth who crossed the river, the lighted bugs shining from the firs and Dolly hanging onto her last breath."

But it wasn't like that at all. When Father and his friends arrived, he came to the cottage. "Mr. McKenzie and the pack ponies and the other members of the party will go ahead and wait for us where the trail takes off for Skyline Ridge. I want you up and ready before dawn. The express-man and I will pick you up and your personal gear and the food Maria has prepared, in his spring wagon. Neal, you will bring Timothy in the top of your backpack. He will follow us, anyway. I have made a list for you to check. This will save several miles of hiking. The girls are not to carry packs, and there will be an extra pony saddled so they can take turns riding when they tire. It's a long, grueling hike at best."

Before dawn Maria's Westcotts were checked and waiting.

The expressman and Father picked them up in the spring wagon, and they crossed the creek. They entered the little forest road. They followed the mad gray-white waters of the Nooksack and met the others, who were waiting farther down the road than they had ever been. Their gear was hastily put on the ponies. They were off. The adventure had begun.

The trail on Skyline climbed gently through summer fir and cedar over long, gentle slopes, the underbrush thick, the duff soft. They passed pristine meadows filled with the fragrance of lupine, violets, Scotch bluebells and buttercups. There was no trace of man. No old campfires, nothing to show man had been here. As the trail on the ridge steepened, they entered the pine forest, with its summer strawberry and its columned trees, and looked down on streams cascading over volcanic rock, and in the distance on each side of the ridge they could see steep green ranges topped by snow. They could look down into deep ravines with glimpses of shining rivers and sapphire lakes.

But the great mountains are shy. They hide behind each other and the bulwarks that protect them. The ranges that divide their glaciers are so overgrown that, though each mile brought the party closer and closer, they had only a glimpse of white through a rare opening.

The girls took turns riding. When they stopped to rest the horses and share the food Maria had prepared for lunch under the trees, it was Tim who taught them that to draw near an animal in the wilderness necessitates one thing—no sudden movement. Below them in a lush wild-flower meadow strolled a doe and a tiny fawn, unaware of man. They watched Tim creep forward slowly until he and the fawn touched noses. That was all. The doe moved off slowly, the fawn following her.

The trail steepened into subalpine fir, white mountain pine and mountain larch. They were in the zone of the rhododendron, phlox and painted brush. They could see deep clear pools fed by dashing streams that came from the mountain snow.

Father said that once all this country had been submerged. The Eocene, Miocene and Pliocene ages were the mountain-building eras. Huge rock jams occurred beneath the water: the surface erupted. The climate changed, freezing the mastodon, the tropical palms, until the glacial period began, the volcanoes building themselves with flow after flow of lava over a period of six million years.

They were weary now, but they must push on to unpack, to tether the ponies so Mr. McKenzie could take them back in the morning. They must put up the tents, gather the firewood, cut the boughs to hold the sleeping bags. The air was thinner now and colder.

"Here we are," Father cried. "Here is where the ridge melted from its abutment to the mountain side. Lead the ponies down into the meadow, Mr. McKenzie. Look at the hummingbirds and the butterflies. That's what we'll call it— Butterfly Meadow." The party left the trail and moved down the ridge, and then it happened, so suddenly it was like a revelation.

Koma Kulshan stood before them. They were on it. No—

there was a steep decline between them, milk-white water streaming from some glaciers they could not yet see.

Cathy said, "What's its name?"

"It's the smallest of the thirteen glaciers on the mountain and it has no name. The mountain is not climbed from this side. I doubt if any man has been up this glacier, but I shall take you."

There was a sudden burst of activity. The men unpacked the ponies. Father chose the spots for the tents. Neal and the boys were set to cutting boughs of white-bark pine for the sleeping bags, the end of no bough larger than a pencil. When the girls' tent was up, father showed them how to weave the bough mattress, six layers thick, the ends carefully tucked in. Jo, the camp tender, set up the mess tent. Keith-Hutton gathered wood for the fire. Ed and Jim carried water from the nearest stream. The horses were tethered for the night. When the fire was hot beneath the sheepherder's stove, Maria put on the coffee and the large pot of meat and vegetables she had precooked at home. She put the sourdough biscuits in the oven. There was no big campfire that first night. The marmots had ceased their whistling. The rosy sunset faded from the mountain until it stood like a silver iceberg from the mist at its base, huge, magnificent, rimmed by stars.

The bough mattresses were soft and all slept well. In the morning when Cathy woke, she pulled on her clothes and crept out of the tent. Mr. McKenzie and the ponies had already gone. The camp tender had the fire going and Neal and Tim were with him. Daylight comes early to a northern mountaintop, and when Cathy had swallowed a cup of cocoa, she and Neal climbed the meadow to the top of the ridge overlooking the decline and watched the sunrise come slowly until the mountain was bathed in amethyst, then in rose, the sun's ray glistening on the snow and ice.

When they returned to the camp the ptarmigan and grouse were feeding. They did not fly away. They had not learned to be afraid of man. They stayed just out of reach.

For two days the men were busy putting the camp in order. Father built a cooler in the stream in which perishables could be kept watertight and fresh. Ed and Jim worked on the woodpile. Neal and Keith-Hutton improvised a dining table from logs and supply boxes.

In Butterfly Meadow was one large snowbank, and the young Westcotts found that by sitting in one of the camp's fry pans they could toboggan down it like the furies themselves, usually ending end-over-end. Neal made the descent on the seat of his pants, using his alpenstock as a brake, Tim in his pack on his back. But once was enough for Timothy who went to sleep by the camp fire and stayed there.

The days slipped by so quickly that the young Westcotts felt themselves trying to hold back time. Not yet—not yet. Each day had its new adventure and delight. On one, Father led the party back along the ridge and onto another—a stiff climb—and from it they could see the largest glacier on the mountain. It was said avalanches here had been so tremendous that hundreds of acres of terrain had been covered with huge blocks of ice, leaving morainelike small mountains. Here they looked upon violence into huge chasms with deep blue shadows, walls smooth as if sliced with a knife, one cone of ice at least a hundred feet high and huge top-heavy seracs so precariously balanced the family were hesitant to breathe lest they fall.

"If you look up that terrible river of ice, Cathy," Father told her, "you will see the sun shining on encrusted yellow, pink and lavender crystals, sulphur fumes from a rift in an ancient crater."

Another day they went on a blueberry hunt and realized suddenly that for the first time they had forgotten Timothy. Neal called him, but he did not come. When they reached Butterfly Meadow, they knew why. At the top of a slender larch sat Tim, on a bough so small it wobbled if he moved. At the base of the tree was a black bear, more curious than savage to see so strange a creature perched above him.

"Timothy not only knows he is a person; he thinks like one," said Father. "He knew perfectly well if he went up a larger tree, the bear would have followed him. Poor little bruin. Timothy kept him from rummaging through our supplies."

The bear ambled off. Tim removed himself to the mess tent.

That night Angela set sprays of heather on the improvised table. The camp tender broiled ham over the open fire. Maria produced a hugh dish of spoon bread and two large blueberry pies from the sheepherder's oven. And when the long twilight had left the mountain and the stars were out, the big camp fire was lighted. It was the chats around the camp fire that Cathy loved. Father was always superb. Tonight he began with Keats: " . . . and all his men/Look'd at each other with wild surmise——/Silent, upon a peak in Darien."

He told in detail about the first ascent of Koma Kulshan by Coleman, the Englishman, aided by the Lummi Indians. He had a way of inspiring other men to talk freely, and the camp fire was always a place of excitement, of humor and, sometimes, of pathos.

The next morning Father and the postmaster were gone before dawn.

"They went down the decline to our small glacier that has no name," said the camp tender. "Mr. Westcott says the weather is ideal. No rains or storms in sight and splendid visibility. If the snow looks good tomorrow, we will make our trip onto the mountain."

When Father and the postmaster returned they were jubilant.

"The glacier has some crevasses, but they do not appear formidable. We will use a rope, however. Above the bergschrund there is snow that should lead us fairly easily to the beginning of the arctic zone. Now I want everyone to bed early because it is a farther climb down the decline than it looks and I want us well on our way before the sun is up. Neal, you take Tim. I don't want him left alone all day. I'm afraid he might come up with a cougar."

Nobody slept well that night. They were up and off at three, before the first crimson rays touched the mountain. For the first time they had to use the rope on the decline. On the eastern side of the glacier, heather still grew in a few protected spots, and stunted, twisted white-bark pine, short and puny, clung tenaciously to the slope, rugged from centuries of assault by snow and tempest. One mountain hemlock, the last tree on the mountain, had grown laterally from a protected ledge, beautiful beyond any other tree, hard, resolute, defying every enemy which had assaulted it. And Keith-Hutton said, "In England it is said King Arthur made his knights search the crags for such trees to make their lances."

They were roped as they started up the small glacier. There were more crevasses than showed from below, but the snow was firm. In one place Maria's feet slipped and Father cut steps with his ice ax. They climbed then with no trouble and passed the basalt at the top of the glacier and onto a rising snow field.

Here they put on goggles and greasepaint, the air thinner now and colder. They came at last to the edge of the arctic zone where no man could live a night. When Keith-Hutton shot his revolver, it made a little puff. There was no echo. There was nothing but snow, lava and basalt, a gale blowing now and frost beginning to form on their brows and eyelashes. Tim stuck his head out of Neal's backpack. Bears were one thing, mountains that frosted a cat's whiskers another. At this moment he was not a cat who thought himself a person. He was a pussycat, and in went his head and stayed there.

Father pointed out the mountains he knew, Church, the Skagit and Baker rivers, the mirrorlike alpine lakes, and the Olympics beyond the shimmer of Puget Sound.

They went down slowly, the snow firm, but when they reached the glacier, they realized it had taken them much longer than they had expected. The sun had been full upon the glaciers, widening the crevasses.

"We won't try it," Father said. "There is a short ridge that will bring us out on a branch of our own ridge. It's sharp, and on the other side is a shale drop. Shale slides easily. We'll go roped. Every step must be carefully taken. Use your alpenstock on the glacier side to help you, and remember we have the rope."

They crossed the ridge very, very carefully. They watched a small shale slide gathering size and speed as it went down into what looked a bottomless chasm. Suddenly, the surgeon, who had never before been on a mountain, cried out, "Stop. I'm going to faint." The postmaster moved instantly to help him. Cathy didn't know a man could be afraid of anything. A little girl, yes. A man, never, and she felt now the tight, compact ball of fear that does not lessen, that does not go away.

Father left the rope and came over to her.

"Cathy, look here." He reached down at her feet and picked a small wild flower growing on the very edge of the ice. "It's an avalanche lily. It's the first living thing we've seen on the mountain. You cannot transplant it. It grows on the very edge of the snow only. Isn't that remarkable?" And Cathy said yes, it was, and they went on.

For the first time in her life, Cathy really prayed. "Your Honor, get us off this ridge and I'll be good for the rest of my life." The instant she thought it, she knew it was wrong. You didn't bargain with His Honor on a mountain or anywhere else. Father said every virtue at its testing point came down to one thing—courage. It was the only thing you could ask.

They reached the ridge with the sudden release of tension. All began to laugh and joke. It was late when they returned to camp, but they were too tired to go directly to their tents. Maria and the camp tender built up the fire, and they ate what was left of the ham and a splendid skillet of corn bread.

"It's a good thing Mr. McKenzie is coming to take us out day after tomorrow," Father said. "Keith-Hutton and I will have to break the law and shoot some ptarmigan. We're giving out of grub."

When the camp fire was lighted that night, they watched the mountain turn to crimson, the alpine lakes to green, to gold and rose. Then the colors faded and the mountain was blanched and lifeless.

"Why does a man climb mountains?" the congressman asked.

"To conquer his fears," said the surgeon. "At least I intend to come back until I do."

"To know himself and his fellow man where both are above all the petty conceits and selfishness of everyday living."

It was Father's turn.

"On a mountain a man stands where there is no life. On his way down he comes upon a small lichen or an avalanche lily. Some power, call it what you will, has taken gas and water and created chlorophyll which sustains all life. Science says now that the creation of our universe was a mere accident, going nowhere, meaning nothing. Yet of all life created on this earth, man alone can marvel. He is greater than any mountain and the stars that rim it. He alone can sacrifice himself unselfishly for an ideal."

The next day Dad and Keith-Hutton went hunting and returned with fossil clams millions of years old that they had found on a nearby smaller ridge, where Skyline Ridge is melted at its abutment.

Maria made the last blueberries into pies and put the birds to stew.

Just as they were sitting down to the last dinner, a horse stopped at the top of the ridge and a forest ranger walked down to the camp.

"Maria," ordered Father quickly, "dump all the clams into the stew and say nothing."

He went forward. "Why, Lee Simms," he said. "You are our first visitor. We invite you to dinner."

"I was hoping you would. Lightning touched off a small fire on Twin Peaks, but it's out now. I saw your fire, and I'm starved."

"Sit down. We're having marmot chowder, skillet bread, and one of Maria's blueberry pies."

"Best marmot chowder I ever had in my life," Lee Simms said with his eyes twinkling. "Where did you find the clams?" They told him.

"We'll name it Chowder Ridge." And so it is known to this day.

"You're welcome to spend the night, Lee."

"No, thank you, sir."

"Then come to dinner first time you're in town."

"I'll do that."

The next morning Mr. McKenzie arrived with the pack ponies. They left with a strange, reverent sadness.

When they reached the cottage, Father said to Cathy, "You're very quiet. What is it?"

"It won't change, will it, Dad?"

"Yes, it will change, and sooner than you think. And when it does I want you to remember it as we saw it this summer."

"I know what you want me to remember. You want me to remember the lovely last tree. That, and the avalanche lily."

And this was the summer of the Snow Mountain.

6. The Shrewd Arrive

The Pettit family came to live in the town that fall. Inured to large families and frequent famines, they had migrated to the East Coast late. Here they prospered.

The grandson, now middle-aged, had put himself through engineering school and helped build the railroad across the plains. He was an able, egotistical but charming man, who combined forces with one of the pioneer mill and timber owners, sufficiently old and weary to welcome so able a partner. Together they acquired and lumbered great tracts of timber.

It was exactly like having royalty take up residence. The Pettit house had no rocking chair each member of the family preferred to all others. Out went the rocking chairs and the old morris chairs. In came the love seats and the wing chairs. Out went the Lone Wolf howling in the snow on some small boy's bedroom wall. Out went Sir Galahad hanging over some small girl's brass bed. The Pettit house was of such imposing elegance that the townswomen began to make sneak trips to Vancouver antiques shops so they too could enter elegance.

Alice, the Pettit daughter, twenty-seven, had been educated in private schools and abroad, and there was about her such a facade of glamour that she made every girl in the town seem ordinary. If she took out a little round box with a French label, removed the top and powdered her nose with a tiny feather puff, no girl could sleep at night until she acquired one exactly like it.

As for Mrs. Prouty of the town, it was obvious she was doomed. Mrs. Prouty arrived yearly at numberless homes, including the Westcotts, a heart-shaped pincushion hung on a ribbon lying sedately on her ample bosom. She stayed several days, sitting on the floor, her mouth full of pins, pinning up the pleated skirts, the camisoles, the petticoats, the wrappers and the very simple party dresses.

There was also a Pettit son, seldom seen because he was being educated at eastern private schools, designed by his creator to make every other boy feel he had nothing on his head but cowlicks, and nothing in it but an empty void. He was a tall and somewhat frail-looking lad, unaccustomed to rough and tumble sports. When he was home long enough to attend one of the dances at the very modest, very small country club, his father did not lend him the Model T for the evening, and he did not pick up two other couples and take them and bring them home. He was the only boy in town with a car of his own, and proud the girl asked to share it.

When the new lumber combine became so large, Dad Westcott lost one of his best clients. A Seattle lawyer replaced him. When Mr. Pettit controlled the leading bank, a man from the East arrived to manage it, and Mr. Huggins, who had done some kindness for practically everyone in the town and the county, found work elsewhere.

There were some who admired the Pettits extravagantly. And others who remained totally unimpressed. Mary Lawrence of the thirteen-million-dollar Lawrence family was one of them. On cold mornings she still went to school with a disreputable old stocking cap pulled over her ears and let the jibes fall. When Mr. Lawrence died, the family closed the old hotel and moved to Portland. The young of the town missed the hazardous, heavenly marble floors. Cathy missed Mr. Ben's escorting her and Mary in their bunny-rabbit slippers and flannel nighties to the room of their choice. Years later when a woman would return to the town after a long absence and somebody would have a luncheon for her, there was always someone who cried loudly, "I remember you. You were the one who fell down the stairs and broke your ankle at the Lawrence party and ruined the day." As for Cathy, she spoke of Mr. Ben all her life. "Your Honor, wherever he is, lead him down the dark spooky halls of life and tuck him in gently."

Another citizen equally unimpressed by the Pettits was, strangely enough, Mrs. Beanor.

"Don't you think it is strange our new American princess is unmarried at twenty-seven?" she asked Mrs. Westcott casually.

"She's looking for some young man who can support her in the manner to which she has become accustomed."

"Well, she's found him. In Seattle. He's the son of a fine

but financially modest family. He put himself through Harvard Law School and has a brilliant future with a New York firm. He's serious, of course. Knows very little about girls. He's never had time to play, though there is one girl everybody has expected him to marry who, compared to Miss Pettit, must seem suddenly very plain. Wherever he goes to lunch, there is Alice Pettit at the next table. I'll say one thing for him. He is struggling on the hook. Evidently, Alice Pettit put it right to him, and he said no, he'd like to think it over. Do you know what she did? She ordered her wedding dress, announced the engagement, and now he marries her or jilts her so conspicuously he looks like a fool. My dear aunt and uncle—Mr. and Mrs. Peter Rabbit, I believe you called them—are perhaps a bit provincial. They are also incapable of pulling a thing like this."

"Mrs. Beanor, I do believe you are gossiping."

"Mr. Westcott, for the first time I am beginning to feel like a westerner."

Very soon Mr. Pettit became the town's most prominent citizen. He even took an interest in the Koma Kulshan National Forest which Father and his mountaineering friends had worked so hard to establish. It was he who announced it must be managed for the greatest good of the most people, and who pulled sufficient strings to get the little forest road widened a little and a small hotel chalet built next to one of the sapphire lakes near Shuksan.

"Oh, Dad," Cathy said. "They'll ruin it."

"In the West, Cathy, where there are great natural resources, the shrewd have always followed the pioneer. The pioneers built this country. They were generous to a fault, and they were naive. As a country, we still are. But our Cascades will be difficult to ruin."

The next summer the family made its last trip to the mountains, Keith-Hutton accompanying them, Tim left under protest on the island.

They went first to Lake Chelan in the very heart of the great glaciers of our country. The lake is one of the deepest canyons in the world, unsurpassed for its sombre grandeur, its marvelous coloring and great cliffs.

Father had never been here and he chose the route carefully. Slowly they made a twenty-five-mile trek up Railroad Creek to Glacier Lake, North Star Park and Cloudy Pass.

Cathy never forgot the look on Father's face when they first saw Glacier Lake. They looked out upon a huge area filled with bright green grass, wild flowers and marvelous trees. Huge peaks, glacier-crowned, rose on every side. To the south, at the southern end of the lake, the waters fell over a five-hundred-foot bluff, the stream coming from a smaller lake above the bluff lying at the end of a glacier four miles long and two miles wide. It was untouched by man.

They climbed west of the lake into North Star Park, and onto the Cascade Divide to Cloudy Pass. Here, to the east, the water flowed to the Columbia River and the Pacific, and to the west, to the Skagit River and Puget Sound. The warm air from the Pacific collided with the crowns of untold mountains, making Cloudy Pass the breeding place of tempests where a blizzard could rise over your head even in August. But they were lucky. They could see the great unknown mountain, Glacier Peak, then visible from no road.

They could see it in all its lonely grandeur, its sister mountains in battle array. Then, from a sky that had been clear two minutes before, a tempest arose directly overhead, and they hurried down.

"We have seen the sublime," Father said.

The Pettit boom was fairly short, if hectic. The old paternalism was gone now. There was trouble in the camps, and though the mill workers were making more than before, there were complaints at the mills. The wilderness receded as Mr. Pettit cut his trees. The little shingle mills which had dotted the deep forests were gone also. The new chalet at Shuksan prospered briefly.

When Mr. Pettit had cut all his timber, he moved quietly to British Columbia to parlay his empire in greener fields. Just before his mill was closed and the last rafts of logs were loaded onto the freighters, he presented to the town a twelve-and-one-half-acre park in honor of "the value of free enterprise."

The boom was over. The next year came the World Depression.

7. The Depression

The town went through the Depression day by day, as in a war. There were no riots. No one jumped out of a window. Those who had gambled in the stock market kept quiet about their losses. It was like a slow death of all the town had been and cherished.

Years later when the subject came up in a group old enough to remember it, the townspeople, like Americans everywhere, spoke of it lightly and often with humor.

"I remember I had holes in my one pair of shoes, so I found a box of old Christmas cards, cut out thick inner liners and walked Happy New Year into the rainy pavements."

"My husband got hold of four cases of tomato soup. We ate tomato soup for five months and nothing else. Do you know, not one of my family complained?"

"We managed to save enough money to buy a chicken for Christmas dinner. When we got it home, we found the butcher had exchanged it for a chicken that was positively green. We took it back. I raved and I ranted. Finally, he gave us another, but you know I had raised such a hullabaloo I didn't enjoy it."

"We wanted to buy some chow mein, which cost thirty-five cents. We had only thirty-four cents. We spent the entire day searching the house. Do you know we never did find that dratted penny."

Was this because time assuaged the pain, as grass grows over the grave? It was not. It was because the Depression generation learned what each generation learns in its own time and in its own way—that there are some things of which no man can speak easily, and sometimes he cannot speak of them at all.

Keith-Hutton had learned it. When Mrs. Beanor said to him, "Tell me how it was in the first war," he replied affably. "Why, of course, Mrs. Beanor. Now, let me see. I remember the German general who surrendered. His orderly pushed him to us in a wheelbarrow and all he had on was his long-legged underwear and a monocle. Funniest thing I ever saw in my life."

The town did not want relief. The word was new and revolting. It wanted work.

Every morning Neal was up before four, mopping out one of the saloons in Old Town, cleaning the vomit from the sidewalk and sweeping out the depot.

Between them Ed and Jim handled three paper routes.

Maria refused her monthly stipend of twenty dollars, though Father always slipped her something for the Sunday collection. She baked homemade bread and pies and sold them.

As for Father, he saved many a man from losing his home by coming up with a clause that read if the owner paid anything at all regularly on the mortgage, he could hold his home. The friend down the street with a bad polio leg dug ditches for those few dollars, but he kept his home.

Father had plenty of clients. The trouble was they could pay him seldom, except sometimes in produce. It was always interesting to see him come home from the office, trying to hold his umbrella with one hand and clutching to his raincoat a sack with something alive and kicking.

Once it was three young chickens whom Cathy named Archibald, Nicodemus and Icabod. What a meal they would make! But when they were large enough for the roasting pan, Maria was such a chicken herself she could not cut off their heads. A drifter from Hooverville, which was on the beach under the Old Town street, came to ask a handout and volunteered to dispatch the chickens and clean them too, "without a squawk, Madam," if she would give him one for the communal pot to simmer with the potato peels the Hooverville residents snatched from the seagulls. He did this well and later assisted with the demise of innumerable rabbits, but Dad noticed that on the gate he always left a mark on the fence in the new language of the drifters—"Stop here. Suckers"—which must be carefully scrubbed off to keep down the overhead.

The chalet near the lovely alpine lake at Shuksan burned and was not replaced. Lee Simms, the ranger, said Mr. McKenzie had put his cayuse ponies out to graze for a living. No one went to the little settlement that summer. Nobody could afford it, simple as it was.

Two banks closed their doors for a time, but the one

operated by Mr. Pettit's man from the East did not close. The manager was a stranger. It did not bother him to turn down a loan to an old and trusted customer, or to pick up stump farms for taxes or on foreclosures. Mr. Pettit was still parlaying his empire.

Cathy, Angela and Neal were all in high school now. The Methodists and the Reverend McCarthy had broadened sufficiently to permit the first dance in the high-school gym. Cathy wore a sweet dimity made by Mrs. Prouty. Angela removed the blue draperies from her bedroom, instructed Maria and Cathy in draping, pinning and sewing them upon her, and dazzled the beholders almost as much as had the departed ex-Miss Pettit. When Angela and Cathy got home, they unsewed Angela, pressed the draperies and rehung them.

In some strange way it was still a winter of content. There were no music lessons. No stage plays came this year. At Christmas the tree was cut as usual with Neal's tomahawk, though the family had to walk farther to find it. Mrs. Beanor was asked to dinner and Keith-Hutton came over, of course. He brought Maria a small Wedgewood pitcher, Angela a Dresden compote, Cathy a silver coffeepot and Mrs. Beanor a Sheffield tray.

"They were my mother's. I am going home."

"Oh, no."

"Yes. You know, of course, that almost my whole generation was killed in the World War. I lost my two brothers, many of my friends. My uncle, who is a widower, lost his only child, a son, heir to the old manor estate in Somerset. I think my uncle tried to be kind to me, but in his eyes there was a look which made me feel he was thinking, 'Why couldn't it have been this one instead of my Robert?' My mother is seriously ill. She is an artist, a good one, and has lived many years in Florence. I will go to her and stay as long as she needs me. My uncle plans to marry again and has asked me to put the old manor grounds in order. I think I owe him that."

"But what of your place on the island?"

"Mr. Pettit's bank manager will take it off my hands for enough to get me home, and a bit more."

Keith-Hutton stayed with them a week, and every day they dreaded the final good-bye. It didn't happen. Father came home from the office one night and announced simply, "Keith-Hutton left today."

"But, Dad, he didn't say good-bye."

"He couldn't. He sent you all his love." And they knew a piece of their youth had gone with him.

Harsh necessity had raised her ugly head, and she changed some people. When Roosevelt was elected president, Hoover became the nation's whipping boy, even though he was the only president to give up a year's salary to help balance the budget and had planned reforms Mr. Roosevelt initiated as his own.

Father ran for the superior court that year, and another attorney, hitherto honest, stumped the county telling the Catholics Father was a rabid Protestant, and the Protestants he was a rabid Catholic. Father lost by 173 votes.

"To be expected," he said calmly, but he looked a little

older now, and for the first time his wiry, springy mountaineer's stride slowed noticeably.

But home was still home, tight unto itself, close, warm,
and unfailing. At night the family still gathered in the big old
room, each one with his homework or a book.

"Dad, what does *inimical* mean?" Cathy would ask, and
Father would answer, "Cathy, you're taking Latin now.
Figure it out for yourself. Take it to its roots. *In* means 'not.'
Amicus means 'friend.' Hence *inimical* means 'unfriendly.' "

One night she asked him if he'd help her write a sonnet,
and he said no, he wouldn't, but while she was writing, he
would write one just for her.

First, he looked up sonnet in the dictionary.

"It's made up of fourteen decasyllabic lines," he announced. "Donne said, 'he is a fool who cannot make one
sonnet and he is mad which maketh two.' Something tells me
this will be my only sonnet."

"Are you going to read it to me?" asked Cathy when she
had finished hers.

"I am not. I am still working."

Many a night that winter Father got out the old family
records collected by his great-great-grandfather and read
them bits that tolled in the mind like bells.

" 'I promise to pay enough deer skins well dressed to make
a Comon man a pare of ample briches.' Our first document
and don't tell me it was not by one Scot brother to another."

"Find one for me, Dad," Cathy said.

"Here's one. Your grandmother, eight greats, I think, had
two boys fighting with Washington. She knew they were
hungry and ill-clad. She spun cloth, made clothes, collected
food and with her daughter set out to find the Army. She had

to hide in a cellar in Germantown, but finally reached Washington's headquarters. He himself very courteously escorted her to the boys' tent. Later, one of them was captured by the British and through a guard she got food to him and saved his life."

"She's for me," said Cathy.

"With scars on both knees, sliding in the cellar?"

"Dad, I'm too big for that now."

"Mrs. Beanor will be delighted to hear it."

"Go on, Dad."

"Well, there was cholera. Nobody knew then it was caused from an infected well in England and brought by boat. It was passed by riverboat across much of the continent. A third of the population would die in about four days. Most of the rest would flee. Grass grew in the streets. But there were always some who stayed to nurse the sick and bury the dead."

"Tell us one for us, Dad," said Ed and Jim.

"All right. I know a good one. After the Revolution several different branches of the family moved over the old oxtrail into land opened in Ohio. They had a hard time with Indians. Two little girls were stolen and never recovered. These were people who had prospered, and they bought large tracts of land and built the first log cabins of the country from their own trees. In about 1830 they used the log cabins for summer kitchens and built fine big houses, some still standing and in use."

"Then what, Dad?"

"The cotton crops in the South went bad, and the large influential plantations that used many slaves were forced to sell them, separating families. This was when the black

Americans made their first heroic break for freedom. With the help of a minister and his six sons, they crossed the river from Kentucky and came up the road where our various ancestors had their farms. They were all against slavery, but they were not wild-eyed abolitionists. They just couldn't stand having runaway slaves hiding in their corncribs and barns, pursued by posses and dogs. Boys in their teens were marvelously ingenious. If a horse of the posse threw a shoe, the forge was always cold; the proper tools were missing. If it were evening one of our great-grandmothers would invite the posse in and feed them well. After supper there were always family prayers, and her husband would get everyone down on his knees and pray and pray and pray, an elderly relative with a cane keeping a watchful eye on the children, and if one showed any signs of giggling—that would be you, Cathy—she would tap her gently on the noggin. Meanwhile, one of the boys, on an unshod pony, would lead the slaves up the dark road, the slaves following the hoofbeats, to the next hiding place."

"We would have liked that."

"It was dangerous. Nothing was written down. At the university in Ohio, long ago, there was a history professor who noticed that every time he came to the underground railroad his classes came awake because their families had been involved. Do you know what he did? For forty summers with horse and carriage he retraced the old routes, collecting all the facts from the old who remembered them."

"Father," said Cathy, "in Montana didn't we treat the Indians badly?"

"We did, indeed. We'll save that for another night."

But when Father spoke of Montana, his voice changed, as does a man's voice when he speaks of a woman he has deeply loved.

"I remember," he said slowly, "the time the Sioux came into Helena, fine tall men they were, too, if a bit tipsy. They went into the largest store, bought all the corsets, put them over their own clothes, and out they came. In two minutes there wasn't a woman on the streets."

He laughed and he said, "And I remember when I hired a rig and took Emily for a ride across the prairie and we bumped into a junkman picking up buffalo bones to sell as fertilizer for three dollars a ton. Nobody who lived through those days can ever forget them. When the first settlers arrived, there were millions of buffaloes. Nobody dreamed we could exterminate them, but we did in a very few years."

"Maria," said Cathy, when the rest of the family had gone to bed, "if Father loved Montana so much, why did he leave it?"

"Because in the wars of the copper kings, which went on and on and on, adventure turned to greed. He was offered a high political office if he would accept a bribe and change his stand on an important political issue."

"And he wouldn't?"

"Cathy, you ought to know him well enough by this time to know he wouldn't."

8. Father's Death

Father made a trip to the country that winter to make a speech for the Republicans. In a bad storm the car skidded into a stump, and he suffered a severe blow to the head. At first it didn't appear too serious, but presently it was obvious he was changing. He was forgetful. He stumbled. Finally, he suffered a stroke. The doctor found a sunken place in his thick wavy gray hair and said he was afraid there was serious brain damage. Dr. Briggs possessed the only X ray in town, large as an upright piano, excellent on arms and legs and very little else. In Boston there was a famous brain surgeon, but Boston might as well have been in deepest Africa.

The family brought Father home from the hospital and took care of him as all families did, then. His office was closed. His law books were sold. Maria stayed on.

One night he wept and called for Nora. When Cathy asked Maria who was Nora, Maria said she had been Father's little sister who had died of cholera when she was three. He had never mentioned her, yet all these years he had carried her memory in his heart, and Cathy wondered now if children ever understood their parents at all.

Toward the end he had a few lucid moments. He said, "I would give my heart's blood to have taken better care of my children."

This was the family's first experience of death. Angela could not stay in the room. Maria was there with her rosary, a tower of strength. Neal and the twins were steadfast, and, of course, Cathy.

When the last day came and they could see only the whites of his eyes, he called for Emily.

Father's funeral was one of the largest ever held in the town, conducted by the Reverend McCarthy at Father's request. Quite a number of the Lummi tribe attended. The forest rangers came in from the mountains. The mountaineers from Portland and Seattle, and even from Canada, attended. Mr. McCarthy said all the customary prayers. Toward the end he read the thirteenth Psalm, Father's favorite. "He lived it," he said. "He was a man of absolute integrity. We have never had too many like him. Just barely enough. We shall never forget him."

When the family returned to the big old house, there was Father's rocking chair, his smoking jacket with the worn spots on the elbows, the thin silver disc on his key chain, his name worn because he had had a habit of rubbing it as he talked. Already they were trying to remember exactly how he had looked, every mannerism, each nuance of his voice.

Something strange happened when Father died. He stood up like the mountains in his own place in his own land. Like the four-masted schooner grounded on the tide flats, he became a symbol of the big broad free spirit of his day. In a kind of repentance, people called him Judge Westcott now. "When Judge Westcott lived," they said, "Judge Westcott would have spoken out. Do you remember how fair he was?"

Father had wished to be cremated, which was unusual then. Lee Simms, the forest ranger, and Neal and the twins took the urn bearing his ashes over the Skyline Trail and buried them under the alpine hemlock near the little glacier that had no name. Lee said, "No man lies in a place more truly his own." Neal said, "Your Honor, we give him back to you with gratitude."

One day when Cathy was sorting out his things to be saved or given away, she came on the sonnet he had written while she was writing on hers. The first fourteen lines had not pleased him and he had scribbled them out. Six lines remained:

A scroll I sought, and strewed thereon a sonnet
Of sweetest pearls that choired their joys upon it
And lured for me rich carnival of dreams.
But, oh, my daughter sweet, when morning came
My scroll was blank except where bright gleams
"I love you, dear." These words alone remain.

                                        J. W.

She showed it to no one. She put it away with the family records. All her life she took out the little poem and peeked at it, but she could not read it, lest she break her heart all over again.

When Father's estate was settled, it proved pitifully small. The house was paid for. There was one small insurance policy. The money Neal's father had left in an eastern bank for his education was paid him.

Cathy carried extra work so she could get through high school, enter the Normal and teach. Angela worked half a day in the public library. The twins carried three paper routes. Since they could not pay her, Father Ryan made arrangements for Maria to enter the Sisters of St. Joseph in New Jersey.

The family went to the train to see Maria off, determined to manage it without a tear.

"Maria, we'll end up in purgatory and who will get us out?"

"Maria, who will untie your apron strings? Who will roll you over a barrel?"

They hugged and they kissed her. Poor Maria. She cried all the way to New Jersey. The Mother Superior wrote Father Ryan that she missed "her Westcotts" so much it was doubtful if she would ever adjust and might have to be sent home. But Maria was made of stern stuff. She stuck it out.

9. *"And the Lads Kept Leaving in the Rain"*

Various conservation corps came to work near the town. Some did excellent work on the roads and trails. To put up a round tower on the highest mountain on Orcas Island one group cut down all the lovely trees and underbrush, so that nothing grew but fireweed.

The Depression was said to be lessening now. But not here. The sawmills were closed. No bright cinder burners glowed in the night sky. What had been the largest canneries in the world were closed because the fleet of steel ships that had gone yearly to Alaska no longer returned with their iced cargo. The fish were canned where caught.

There is a strange depression that hangs over every little town that is no longer in the mainstream of life. The boys whose parents owned the largest stores and businesses stayed on. So did the boys responsible for older and sadder parents, or for young brothers and sisters. The unencumbered drifted away, sure as youth is always sure that all that is important, all that matters, lies far away in some big city.

It was exactly like the old ballad that has come down the centuries from England from other hard times: "And the lads kept leaving in the rain."

Neal talked it over with Cathy, took his inheritance, and with the drifter who had beheaded the chickens rode a freight to California to enter Stanford and get an education for the days Mr. Roosevelt said were on their way.

There never was a student generation quite like those boys from distant small towns who worked their way through a fine university in the Depression. It can hardly be said they went to college at all. They went through it, which is something else. Loners all, living in some small room of a professor's garage, cutting his lawn, trimming his hedge, scrubbing his floors for the room. California was a far richer state than Washington. There were still young people untouched by the Depression, girls in their cashmere sweaters and camel's hair coats, boys on fraternity row who had time and money enough for activities, all destined to remember these roseate years that drew them back to reunions to gambol in the happy pastures of their youth. But not Neal and many others like him. He bicycled three times a day to Palo Alto to wash dishes for his meals. He corrected papers. He signed tuition notes. He went to summer school. He never had a date all the time he was in college. But every month he sent Cathy a small check to help her out, and when he won a five-hundred-dollar scholarship, he sent her half.

Once he fell off his bicycle and cut his knee badly. When he went to the infirmary to have it sewed up, the doctor said he had been working too hard and suggested he go to sea for six months: "You'll have no trouble with the union. Can you row?"

Through Knut Larsen, one of Dad's old clients, first mate on one of the old Dollar boats, he passed his boat test and made two trips to China, first as an ordinary, then as an able-bodied seaman. All his life he never forgot standing in the bow at night in the lovely Sea of Japan, calling out, "The lights are burning brightly, sir." He never forgot the sweet old Chinese sew-sew woman who came right into the fo'castle where the men were dressing, calling "Sew-sew," who washed, ironed and mended their clothes for a few cents, the men bringing her small gifts, showing her pictures of their girls, confiding in her. Neal found more real democracy at sea than at the university, and when he returned he brought a jade ring for Cathy. He was in love with Cathy. He guessed he always had been, but he did not permit himself to brood on it because any future with her was still too far away. This he sensed along with a desperate need to hurry.

Stanford gave Neal what he sought, a fine education. In return he gave it the best he had. Years later he never went back to a reunion. When the alumni magazines arrived, it amused him that the loners like himself never wrote in. It was the same old crowd who filled the pages with their accomplishments, their travel, their sentimental nostalgia.

Once—just once—he worked his way home on a freighter, hitching a ride from Seattle north. When he reached the beloved home Ed and Jim came rushing to meet him, and Tim, now a great-grandfather, managed to lift himself from the polar bear's head and sit on his lap.

"Cathy will be here in a few minutes, Neal," Angela said. She had grown very lovely, with something still and hidden in her face.

He heard Cathy's step on the stair and opened the door.

"Oh, Neal," she said. "I knew you'd come."

In the lovely twilight he and Cathy walked to a secluded spot under the firs on the bank overlooking the Sound, and he slipped the jade ring on her finger. It was like Browning's *Confessions:* "Alas, we loved, sir—used to meet./ How sad and bad and mad it was,/ But then, how it was sweet."

It was perhaps a trifle mad, but not bad enough to lift an eyebrow, and Cathy laughed and said, "Isn't life ironic? Dr. Briggs kept his word. We passed the doctor's book around in the cover of *The Little Shepherd of Kingdom Come.* We couldn't figure out how any of us ever managed to be born. And what good did it do us? I'm teaching, and if you marry me, I lose my job. If you get me pregnant, what would become of us?" What indeed!

"Cathy, listen to me. Mr. Roosevelt didn't end the Depression. It's the new lend-lease. Orders are pouring in for arms and planes. It's going to mean the biggest boom the country's ever had. Not here, perhaps. It may pass by the small forgotten towns. But the big centers of industry are going to pick up the pot of gold at the end of the rainbow and, you know, it scares me a little. Promise you'll wait for me."

"I'll wait for you, Neal."

When he had gone, Cathy went up to the big unfinished

part of the attic where the mountain gear and alpenstocks were still stored, and for the first time she felt that hard core of fear she had felt the time they walked the narrow ridge above the shale and the crevasses.

"I hate war," said Mr. Roosevelt in his fireside chats, as industry flourished. "But if your neighbor's house is on fire, do you not lend him your hose?"

"No American is going to be asked to fight on foreign soil," said Mr. Roosevelt's mellifluous voice, which was exactly what all Americans wanted to hear.

The country was moving ahead again. Neal handed in his thesis and made arrangements to have his diploma in engineering "with distinction" mailed to him. He was going home. Nothing was going to stop him. But something did.

Its name was Pearl Harbor.

Part Two

AM I THE LAST?

10. Neal

Neal enlisted at once, trained as a navigator in California. He helped fly over heavy bombers with the bombsight which England needed so desperately, served as a convoy escort against air and U-boat attack, his plane and crew finally attached to the Eighth Air Force stationed in England. His plane was chosen for missions where precision high-altitude bombing was especially vital. Once, after more than thirty such missions, he sent Cathy a small snapshot of himself and his crew being decorated, looking young, shy and very, very modest. Cathy wrote cheerfully always and told him about the Russian flyers from Alaska who were sent to Keith-Hutton's place on Orcas to rest, a stocky, disciplined, taciturn group, neither friendly nor unfriendly, but greatly taken with the island and its small deer. One, who knew a bit of English, actually smiled and said when the war was over this was where he wanted to live.

The first Christmas Cathy sent Neal a small live fir

trimmed with one hundred tiny presents. Neal shared it with the crew, the men whooping with laughter at the useful, imaginative and funny gifts they all took part in unwrapping.

In 1943, with a hundred and fifty heavy bombers, after careful briefing by a Norwegian commando from the commando center in the north of Scotland close to Seam bridge at the Inverlochy Junction, Neal's plane helped attack a strange plant perched like an eagle's eyrie on a steep mountain cliff in Norway. He did not know it was the Norsk hydrohydrogen electrolysis plant where Germany was making heavy water in a desperate effort to create an atom bomb before the Allies. The weather turned bad, the terrain was difficult, and though they damaged the plant, they did not destroy it. Nevertheless, Germany moved the drums onto a ferry and across a deep lake, planning to take them into Germany, and four Norwegian commandos who, by a miracle of courage, had previously entered and damaged the plant, blew up the ferry over the lake. Neal did not know this was one of the great coups of the war, and when he did, he was proud of his small part and a tremendous admirer of the heroic Norwegian underground.

Once, when socked in by foul weather, he managed two days' leave in Edinburgh.

"I shall bring you here," he wrote Cathy. "We'll walk up the winding hill past the old gray university. I will show you Edinburgh Castle, rebuilt in 700 A.D., and Holyrood, where Mary, Queen of Scots, was born. You will love the moors and hedgerows of white hawthorn, the gorse and whin, the beech trees, the wild rhododendron, and the gardens in front of Princes Street. But one thing I refuse. I won't let you take a bath in the huge tub at my old hotel. I know my tomboy Cathy. You'd fill it to the brim to see if you could float."

On D day Neal and crew went into Normandy, bombing installations and shore defenses. They were part of the terrific bombardment of Brittany and of Cherbourg. When the Germans launched their buzz bombs on London, his plane bombed the caverns near Paris where the bombs were stored, and the launching sites.

In the months before Germany was entered, his plane was chosen for more precision high-altitude bombing in Germany. The team bombed oil and supply depots, communication centers, strategic railroads, U-boat installations, industrial plants and bridges.

On the last flight the plane was damaged by flak; the crew parachuted out and were taken prisoner. Their dog tags, shoes, uniforms, watches, were removed. They were moved by freight car back into Germany and kept in what seemed to be a large old farmhouse with shuttered windows and an enclosed exercise yard. A doctor of sorts set Neal's broken ankle, but he did it so badly Neal was in constant pain. They were not mistreated. They were not even questioned. The thin gruel and black bread were barely enough to keep them alive. Their attendants were old.

Even the young had been called up. It was evident here that everyone was preparing to run the first chance they could manage it.

There is a humor that goes with every fighting man who faces imminent death, and it helped Neal stay sane and survive. They made up jokes and crazy games. Sometimes, on

the rainy nights on the top floor of the old house, they took
turns reciting poems they had learned in school. As they
grew weaker they talked of home. Each, whoever he was,
thought his home the dearest, his countryside the fairest.
Was it still the same? Was Dad Westcott safe under his
wonderful tree? On the mesas of Colorado could you still see
the circles where the Indians had raced their ponies? Did the
children still walk to school through the blooming orange
groves of southern California? On the prairies of Nebraska
were there still marks where the settlers' teams had cut so
deeply nothing had grown over the gashes? And in Ohio, in
Gardener's Hollow, did the buzzards still lay their speckled
eggs in nests made of sticks on the ledges and upchuck in
your face if you drew near? Did the flying gray squirrels still
glide through the oaks?

They were there some months before the Ardennes and
the Battle of the Bulge, and they were lucky, even if they
didn't know it, since this was Germany's final offensive
against the Anglo-Canadian and American armies, and there
were places like Malmédy where American prisoners were
cut down by machine guns and left on the ground.

They could hear the guns coming. They could see the
lights flash from behind the shuttered windows, closer and
closer. Then, one day nobody came to feed them their pitiful
ration. Nobody came at all. The gate to the courtyard was
open. They stumbled out. They were near a concentration
camp and they could see American troops entering it. They
stumbled after them and told them who they were. What he
saw, Neal swore he would never tell anyone. Not the twins.
Not even Cathy.

"Food," they begged. "Food." They were taken to a clearing station, then to a station hospital.

"Only a sip, not too much. Slowly. Slowly."

Later they were flown to a hospital in England. Several of the men had tuberculosis. Neal was more fortunate. He was emaciated and terribly weak. When his strength had been built up sufficiently, the surgeons rebroke his ankle, drained and reset it. Then he was flown to Letterman Hospital in San Francisco. He had been reported missing, but there were too many wounded coming in to start retracing the records and reestablishing his identity in England.

11. You Can't Go Home Again

At Letterman they reduced the cast on his ankle, fattened him, took off his cast, gave him therapy, then a walker and finally a cane.

Meanwhile, all his medical history was gone through: fingerprints, teeth, every scar on his body. He was asked innumerable questions about his early life, dates, places, names, by a middle-aged major in the C.I.D.

Neal had written Cathy as soon as he arrived; the letter returned, address unknown. She had disappeared into thin air as definitely as had he. In the ward other men had girls who had not waited and employers who had promised them old jobs, but did not keep their word.

While he grew well again, fear gnawed at him and he denied it vigorously. Not Cathy. Anybody else, but never Cathy.

One day the major in charge of reestablishing his identity called him into his office.

"There's no doubt about it. You're Neal Herbert. Are you aware you have a small chip off your left front incisor? Also, a small scar under your chin? You got them coming down Church Mountain. A most determined nun, one Sister Marie Vincentia of the Sisters of St. Joseph at Newark, New Jersey, says so. If there is a scar on you she doesn't know about I don't know where it's hiding. The scar on your wrist you have forgotten is where you cut an artery while playing mumblety-peg, aged eleven. She confirms it. Says she took you to Dr. Briggs and held your hand while Dr. Briggs sewed it up. He confirms that also."

He opened a folder and took out some photographs, small, old, square, obviously made with an ancient Brownie.

"Here's one I like," and he held out a picture of Neal with Tim's head poking up from his backpack. "Where was it taken?"

"On a snow bank in Butterfly Meadow off Koma Kulshan."

"And what was the pussycat's name?"

"Timothy, sir, but he didn't know he was a cat. He thought he was a person."

"And the glacier you climbed. What was its name?"

"It had no name."

"Sister Marie Vincentia asks you to see Lee Simms and Mrs. Beanor first, because Mrs. Beanor has something she insists on telling you. Then she wants you to come east and see her. Father Ryan of your town writes that the order is likely to lose one of its best nuns if you don't do it, because she threatens to start west herself. She says you were reported dead, which is not true, and that she has notified Cathy you are alive and Cathy is waiting."

"I didn't think," said Neal slowly, "I was afraid—."

"You were afraid you couldn't go home again. I'm old and I've lived through two wars, and I'll tell you something. Every man goes home again, one way or another. He has to, if only in his mind. Oh—you'll find it changed. You may not even recognize parts of it. It's a queer thing. A man lives his life forward, but he understands himself and his parents and much of what he is by going back. Not to stay, perhaps. To find out what in life he values, both the good and the painful."

He stood up.

"It will take a bit of time to straighten out the money due you while you were imprisoned. The doctors want five more pounds on you. Wolf it down, son. Wolf it down. You'll use a cane for a time, but the doctors feel sure eventually you'll be fit again. You'll check back here in two months."

He grinned.

"By the way, how did a nun happen to live with the Protestant Westcotts?"

"She wasn't a nun. She was a servant. She was known as the Westcotts' Maria. Do you know it wasn't until I was stuck in that farmhouse in Germany that it dawned on me it was the other way around. We were Maria's Westcotts."

"When you come back, I want to hear all about it. It's a bit unusual."

"I promise, sir."

"You better, or I'll spend two months worrying about Sister Marie Vincentia hitchhiking her way across the country to find you."

12. Mrs. Beanor

When Neal left Letterman, Germany had surrendered. Attlee had replaced Churchill. The atom bomb had been dropped on Japan. We had won the war, though there were those who were not sure we had won the peace.

Lee Simms met the train from Seattle, and said. "We'll drive home. I bought the old house when Cathy left. I'm still a bachelor and I rattle around considerably. I have every intention of filling it some day with a family as much like yours as I can manage. Every week Mrs. Beanor comes over and suggests candidates. She'll be waiting for us."

The town looked the same. Koma Kulshan stood in the September sun as beautiful as ever. The islands were the same. But there was a strange quietness now. When the car stopped in front of the house, the simple act of walking up the steps and through the door into the memories, with their deep and poignant love, their sacrifice and pain, took courage.

The books were gone, the polar bear rug, the chest from Sitka. When he went to the window and looked down the Sound, no four-masted sailing ship rested on the tide flats, listing like a crippled bird.

"Here comes Mrs. Beanor," Lee announced. "She's been peeking from behind the lace curtains," and sure enough, Mrs. Beanor came scuttling over. She had changed. She looked older, almost humble.

When she came in, she put her old arms around Neal and said, "Thank God," and he laughed and answered. "Now don't tell me some horrible tramps have been shooting hell-divers on the Sabbath morning?"

"Wasn't I awful? I'm ashamed when I think of it. I was so lonely I would think up reasons to get over here and be asked to dinner so I could be part of life and youth for a little while."

They sat down in the old living room, Mrs. Beanor's hands moving nervously.

"Neal, there is something I must tell you. When Maria left, you went away to college and the war began, Cathy knew what she was up against. All over the country, daughters knew, not just in the small forgotten towns. They were trapped. They were the ones who took care of parents, younger brothers and sisters. They knew what nobody ever mentions about the Depression. Their chances to marry until they were thirty-eight or forty, or ever, were small indeed. It was true of many young men also. Angela knew. Especially Angela."

"You are sure?"

"Who could be more sure than the neighborhood snoop? Cathy did not play the odious role of the family martyr. None of that nonsense. She was gallant. I remember once I asked Dad Westcott what was gallantry, and he said it was the ability to accept adversity not only with courage but with grace, knowing you were giving up years of your life youth considers its own, that could not be given back."

"Yes, I know."

"When you were reported missing, Cathy never faltered. 'He's alive,' she said. 'I just know it.' But there was a change in Angela. She worked mornings at the library, spending what little money she made on herself. She had grown very lovely. Sometimes, peeking out of my lace curtains when Cathy was teaching and the twins were at school, I would see young Pettit's car draw in from Vancouver, and the two of them would go off together. He was through college now and the growing Pettit empire included a fine estate in Westchester, New York. One day Cathy came to my house and said Angela and young Pettit had told her the Army had sent word of your death. I remember I asked if they had proof, and she said yes, they had shown her a telegram. She spoke so quietly, as if—as if—her life had ended. The next day, while Cathy was at work, Angela packed her things and went to Vancouver to be married. Without a word, without a good-bye. She even bought clothes and left the bills for Cathy to pay. Angela, of whom I had never had the slightest doubt, and the new shrewd people thought it was very clever of her to get away. It was 'Poor Cathy,' this, and 'Poor Cathy,' that, and that is when I did it."

"Did what, Mrs. Beanor?"

"I wrote Keith-Hutton and told him you had been re-ported dead and I asked him to come home. He had sent me a note at Christmas that he had stayed with his mother in Florence until her death and then gone to his uncle's estate in Somerset, who had married again and managed to produce an heir. He said he missed us."

"Did he answer?"

"No, he came. He had no difficulty. He is an American citizen. He had brought with him a fifteenth-century oil panel by Alessio Baldovinetti, left him by his mother. This he had sold in the East for a sizable amount. One evening, when Cathy and the twins came home from work and school, he was on the front porch, smoking his pipe. Of course, I did not go over, but I did manage to see him put down his pipe and hold out his arms and just gather them in, and I heard him say, 'Now, now, none of that. We are still a family.' "

She paused.

"The next day a van arrived and took all the furniture. Keith-Hutton packed a car with the family's personal effects. The last thing he did was walk over and tell me good-bye. He said that as far as he could find out, you were reported missing somewhere in Germany before the Bulge. He said the Army had not reported you dead. He said, 'Now, Mrs. Beanor, listen carefully. It is highly possible he'll turn up. We are going to find ourselves a new home. There are too many memories here. If Neal returns, I want you to make it clear to him that I am not going to take his place. I am going to do my best to take Dad Westcott's place. I need them. They need me. I'll let Maria know where we settle,' and he took my old faded face between his hands and kissed me, and he said, 'Bless you for bringing me home.' "

The next day Lee Simms drove Neal to the settlement in the last valley tucked amid the ranges. The logging train was no more. The stump farms were gone; mechanical wonders developed since the beginning of the war twirled out huge stumps on high lines. When he saw the prosperous farms, their fields filled with fine dairy herds, Neal wondered if any of them still belonged to the farmers who had spilled out their guts trying to clear their land, only to lose it in the Depression. There were no shingle mills, no skid roads.

When they reached the entrance to what had been the little settlement, Neal knew for the first time that memory can be fallible. It had changed so greatly he was at first totally disoriented. The old hotel, the saloons, the little cottage they had always rented, all were gone. The store was still there and one house he remembered, strangely enough, turned around.

They stopped at the ranger station and got a map. Everything had a name. They crossed the new bridge across Glacier Creek, and when they came to a sign that read CHURCH MOUNTAIN VIEWPOINT, they stopped and got out. All these years Neal had carried in his wallet a picture he had taken with his Brownie Kodak of the mountain with its beautiful serrated top, looking a mile away. He had forgotten entirely how it towered above them, and for the first time he wondered why they had been no more paralyzed by fear than is the Indian child playing in his own village.

The little forest road was wider, but the giant trees still

stood, the sun still filtered down in its eerie light, the road still followed the mad white glacial waters of the Nooksack. But where were the children on the cayuse ponies that rode like young Indians? Where had they gone?

"Am I the last?" he asked himself. "Am I the last to even remember them?"

They drove to Picture Lake close to Shuksan. They could not see Koma Kulshan. The road had covered the magnificent fall flowers with dust. Where it rose following a ridge to a place from which Koma Kulshan could be seen, a huge snowplow stopped in defeat, the road, covered with dust, facing a huge snowbank fifty feet high, sliced clean as a piece of angel cake. In some strange way Neal felt an immense relief that Kulshan, which held so much of his youth, still belonged to itself.

"Do you suppose anybody has been up our little glacier?"

"I doubt it. The place you found the clams is officially named Chowder Ridge. But no one attempts to climb Kulshan from that side. The last time I was there even Butterfly Meadow showed very few camp fires. The ptarmigan and grouse still flutter close to your feet."

On the way back Neal noticed that one side of Church Mountain had been logged.

"Clear cut," Lee explained. "They took off every single tree and see how the heavy rains have washed the rocks. Nothing will grow there for many, many, many years. The various mountain clubs are attempting, and with success, to declare new portions of the Cascades a wilderness area. No roads permitted. Roads ruin a wilderness. The trouble is that what logging shall be permitted in the deep valleys is decided by the head forester. Congress has nothing to say about it. If the top forester is interested in conservation, he is careful, but if he listens to the logging lobbyists, it is another matter. In another ten years we may have a growing problem to save even a small percent of our marvelous mountains. The large animals, of course, have moved on into the farther mountains."

On the way back they came to one place in the road from which they could see Kulshan, but already it was so far away it was remote in its magnificence.

That night Neal and Lee Simms stood in the big upstairs windows and watched the twilight come to the bay.

"That Stanford president was right," Lee said. "Some salmon are returning to the islands after all these years, Oh— not the great runs of the past, but enough to provide a living for a few fishermen."

They could see the lights coming on in the houses on the hills, the lights on the masts of the fishing boats slipping in from the islands. The air was misty now, filled with raindrops not yet fallen, only felt. This had not changed, and if you grow up in a small town on the sea, you never forget the quiet peace of it. It is unchanging and unchangeable. It is like the close war buddy who has been through hell with you. You may not meet him again for years, but when you do, he is as you left him, the bond lasting, constant, and like no other.

The next day Neal took the train for New Jersey.

13. Sister Marie Vincentia

When Neal arrived in New Jersey he called the mother house and told the Mother Superior who he was and asked permission to see Sister Marie Vincentia. She asked him to luncheon the next day.

The Mother Superior was the only woman at the table. The other two guests were men of the Church. The sisters served the meal. Neal was vastly uneasy at the stranger who had been Maria, who scarcely looked at him, as she served his food with care and exactitude.

When luncheon was over, the Mother Superior said to him, "I know you and Sister Marie Vincentia have much to say to each other," and she led him into a small parlor and asked him to be seated. "She will be here at once."

The door opened and she entered. Was this all that was left of so large a part of his youth, this woman in the black habit, the stiff white wimple, the white bandeau holding the coif across the brow, the crucifix on her breast, and over her head the long black veil, the ends of which hid her hands?

He stood up in desperation. He went toward her slowly, using his cane. When he spoke, he heard his voice saying words that surprised him.

"Maria, do you remember when I used to tease you about purgatory in which you believed and we did not? I have come from there."

And lo—the miracle! It was exactly like the morning long ago in the last summer of childhood when the children had stood in the clearing, watching Church Mountain, the light coming, slowly the truth totally revealed. She simply held out her arms and drew him to her as she had done the time he had cut his wrist badly and she had held the pressure point all the way to the doctor and told him how brave he was. And suddenly he was spilling it out, the sights he had sworn never, never to tell anybody, the emaciated rows of bodies seven hundred feet long, sixteen feet wide, stacked like cordwood, the small holes into which had been stuffed the bodies of little children, even of infants. The little girl of fourteen who had not yet been killed, as dazed as he, holding in her hand a bar of soap and on it in German the one word: *JEW*. Yes, even the stench, the unbelievable stench.

Maria said, "There. It is out now. It is done. I have taken if from you and I will carry it. It is part of my calling. It is a kind of intercession. Sit down beside me. I have something to tell you. It is about Angela."

"Maria, I cannot forgive her and young Pettit for reporting to Cathy I had been pronounced dead when it wasn't true. Every night I have the same horrible dream. I dream I meet her on Koma Kulshan on the edge of the arctic zone, where the sounds are muffled and eerie. Each time I push her off the mountain, and she slips over the side without a sound, and I am happy."

"Life has already pushed her off the mountain, Neal. She is one of those women who cannot face life without marrying. To escape it she was willing to hate all she had once loved, even with complete betrayal, anything at all to get away, to live." She was quiet for a moment.

"I went to see her once. She lives on an elegant estate in Westchester with a butler, a cook, a maid and a chauffeur. I asked the maid to send up my name. 'Tell her Maria is here.' She was gone a long time. When she came down, she said loudly, 'Madam says to tell you she is not at home.' She was a Jamaican Negress with a lovely English voice, and she took hold of my sleeve and she said very softly, 'Sister, forgive her. Mr. Pettit did not tell her that his mother's family carry hemophilia. Already, the sadness is on her face.'"

"The men are bleeders and there is no cure."

"Don't go near her. You will say things you will regret and so will she. Each day I pray that some day she will come back to us, but it must be in her own time, when she can forgive herself."

He told her quickly of Mrs. Beanor, of Lee Simms and the changes in the mountain and the town.

"Maria, why do you think Dad Westcott climbed mountains? What did he seek?"

"To know himself and life. The hardship, the patience, the

effort, the fear. That instant's glimpse of the snow beyond. That moment on the last ridge which was like a revelation. Each generation does this in its own way. But the one thing I think he loved most was looking down at the ingredients with which God created all that lives. The first tiny lichen. The avalanche lily blooming on the very edge of the snow. The moment when he knew again that of all living things man is the only one who can know reverence and seek its meaning."

He smiled. "I'll tell you a secret, Maria. To me Heaven is . . ."

"A mountain meadow," she said quickly, "with Tim touching noses with the little fawn. Oh, Neal, we had everything, didn't we? Except, of course, one thing."

"Money, and that doesn't seem very important now."

She stood up. She took out a small paper and tucked it in his hand. "Here is Cathy's address. Go to it slowly. It will teach you much of your country and your family. Too much, too soon; too little, too late! We have made many mistakes, but what else can a people do who enter a continent of which they know almost nothing?"

"I will not let you go unless you bless me."

"I have blessed you every day of your life since you came to us, that sad boy who could not smile, carrying a tomahawk and a pussycat." And she was gone.

In the hall the Mother Superior was waiting, her intelligent eyes on Neal's face. She seemed pleased at what she saw.

"Thank you," he said humbly and cautiously. "Mother

Superior, do you suppose that someday at your choosing Sister Marie Vincentia could come home to visit her Westcotts?"

"My son, I think it might be arranged. In fact, I have promised it."

Outside he took out the paper. On it were written two words—Glen, Montana.

14. And The Sky Came Down All Around, All Around

On the Great Northern Railroad crossing North Dakota, it seemed to Neal his father was waiting for him in Helena. Too young for tragedy, he had blotted his father's memory out of his mind when Tim had taken it upon himself to find them a new home with the Westcotts. Now memory was back, poignant and sharp. He could remember the time his father had taken him to see what Lewis and Clark called The Gates of the Mountains. He could remember the time the Crow had come to Helena with ponies gentled for the children, each father eager to choose the very best for his son. When it had come Father's turn, he had looked at the Crow and said slowly, "You know them, Chief. It will be my boy's first pony. I want him to take care of him and love him. I'll be happy to take the one you choose," and something had flickered across the Crow's proud face and he had said, "This one." He was the best of all and Neal named him Prince. Sometimes of a summer evening, when his father had to make a call—in his carriage, of course—Neal would go along on Prince to a ranch some distance from town. He remembered the time his father had done emergency surgery on the kitchen table, the family helping, and Father had asked him to hold the lamp while he removed a small boy's finger burned in a branding fire. The lad's father gave the chloroform, and when the finger was removed, Neal had been afraid he was going to be sick. When they had left, his father had said to him, "There was a bit of wobblement with the lamp, but I am proud of you, son." He wished he had told his father then that he loved him. Why was it a man seldom says the important words until it is too late? He was feeling lonely when an older man asked if he might sit with him.

"I'm Nat Burke," he said. "I'm a friend of Keith-Hutton's. When Ed and Jim were still in school he paid me to help him build his ranch. I was glad to do it. I lost two boys at Anzio. I married again and have Thad whose mother died when he was six. We've found it a bit hard to adjust. I bought a surplus gooney bird from one of the boys back from the war. We're looking for a piece of land. Now that Ed and Jim are able to take over, I am going to sell my land in Dakota. Thad and I are looking for property in Montana where my interest in wheat and Thad's interest in quarter horses will combine."

"Found it yet?"

"No. Keith-Hutton's helping me. He's an expert on fine horses. There are little towns all through the prairies now— far from each other—the roads terrible. Each town has a small landing strip and if it doesn't you can always land in a cabbage patch. There are no passenger or cargo planes as yet. Want to come along and have a look?"

They started at Bismarck, where Nat's gooney bird was waiting, and a doctor, visibly agitated.

"Thank God you came, Nat. The kids at the Fort Peck reservation have impetigo again and, on top of that, a fierce outbreak of whooping cough. If I don't get there in a hurry with pertussin, no Assiniboine or Sioux chief will get a wink of sleep in a month."

"Hop in, doc."

They dropped him at Poplar. They flew over the million-acre reservation, over the great Peck Dam, in which they could see reflected the wings of their plane and a huge band of geese flying south.

"See those rolling hills?" Nat said. "They are terraces cut by buffalo hooves, and the trails led down to the water holes. But when the first herds of cattle were brought in by eastern money, by English and Scotch companies, the land was overgrazed. They bred the cattle, so they froze in the bad winters, the losses heartbreaking. But it was the sodbusters that ruined it. They came with the building of Hill's railroad. Free land for the asking! They plowed ten inches deep. The thistles moved in. So did the locusts and the grasshoppers. The drought turned the rich topsoil to dust and blew into the Dakotas. In the Depression the government took a page from Alberta's history and taught contour and strip farming, shelter breaks and diversification."

It was like one of those wonderful days of Neal's childhood, which he could never remember quite accurately. The sky came down all around, all around. It was like flying in an endless sea with a hundred variations of color, the winds of the sea, the strange odors born upward, the great clouds that seemed in constant motion above an immensity of land that for hundreds of miles showed not a ribbon of road, not a trace that man had been daring enough to come there and brave enough to stay.

The little towns Neal mixed up badly. Was it Broadus or Roundup? Was it Wisbaux or Circle? Was it Eklaka or Lone Deer? They dropped off sheep-dip, baby bottles for mother-less lambs. They dropped off tools, axes, saws, repaired harvester parts. They dropped off sulfa for wheezy horses, worm medicine, distemper vaccines and gall salves. In one strange place of variegated rock and stunted trees they saw a large bank of antelope running swiftly below them.

"We're coming down soon at Dillon. Your family's ranch is at Glen, twenty miles up the road. We've crossed the state and it's taken us most of the day. The family's been driving their cattle to the high range in the Beaverhead National Forest."

"How do you know?"

"Because you called Sister Marie Vincentia to tell her good-bye and which day you were leaving and how. She called Keith-Hutton, and he caught me in North Dakota. He knew Cathy would come home first, and he wanted you two to meet alone. The house will be open. It's never locked. Even the neighbors want you to have a real homecoming."

"Nat, will I see you again?"

"You will, indeed. Where there are only a bit more than

four people per square mile, we have a tendency to look out for one another."

They were down now. A man in a truck said, "Sure, Nat, I'll drop him off. Be glad to."

Now Neal was passing through country as different from the plains as could be imagined. He saw the Western College of Education at Dillon. He saw two streets of old one-room log cabins where pensioned cowhands and herders still lived. He saw great sweeps of valleys and mountains, shadows of clouds on sage, green alfalfa and hay. He saw children racing their ponies along a dirt road lined with cottonwoods. He saw lovely old houses, one of native brick with a tower room at the top, whose original owner had owned the first cattle herd driven from California.

Glen was a post office combined with a gas station and a store.

"The ranch is two miles up this road. I'll be glad to take you there."

"I'll walk it, and thank you."

He had lost his cane, but he didn't seem to need it. He saw the house. The original, which was now the lower floor, had been built of logs. White clapboard additions had been built. There was a flowered lawn, a large vegetable garden, corrals and cattle pens. There was no barn. The door was unlocked. When he went into the kitchen, he knew the family was expected this day because on the table waited pies and rolls and dishes of food, warm to the touch.

The lower floor, the logs still visible, belonged, obviously, to Ed and Jim. He walked slowly into the living room. There was the polar bear, the red camphor-wood chest. On the mantel was the ivory cribbage board and Cathy's little stand-up rabbits. And, of course, the books! Even the little red books, the *What Every Young Man Should Know* books, over which they had laughed and later despaired. He could tell Cathy's room by the snapshots of Dad Westcott and himself, Tim in his backpack. He could tell the spare room—very, very orderly. He could tell Keith-Hutton's room by his mother's photograph and an excellent watercolor, surely done by her. At the top of the house he found his own room, the tomahawk on the wall, and on the foot of the bed a cat which surely must be Tim's great-grandson.

He went outside to watch.

"Come now," he whispered. "Come now." Presently, he saw her, coming fast and alone in a pickup, hurrying to a moment for which she had been waiting a very long time.

When she reached the corral, he walked forward quietly.

"Cathy," he called softly. "Cathy." He knew what she would answer. He had called her name as a man calls the name of the woman he loves when he comes home at night, spent, exhausted. Has his whole world fallen around him? Does he need her for some awful emergency? No. He just wants to know she is there. Yet these were the words he wished to hear at the end of life, at the very end.

She was older; she was thinner. On her face was a new and stronger look, as on his own. She came toward him.

She said, "Here I am, darling. Here I am," and he knew he was home.

That evening when Keith-Hutton and Ed and Jim came down from the high range, Cathy and Neal had the old ivory napkin rings at all the proper places, the food hot, the coffee made. Everybody laughed and talked at once, and Cathy cried just a little. And the questions!

Neal wanted to know how they had found this place and recognized it as home. Because there was space to swing your arms and expand your soul. That was how. Because the people were few, friendly and free of pettiness and class distinction. At Twin Bridges they had met a woman whose husband had been a famous mining engineer, and who had stayed on after his death and sold ranches. In the back of her car she always carried a box of bones for the dogs, a box of candy for the children and, having disposed of two ranch hazards, she had driven them over the country until they had found this house and the middle range which adjoined it. Ed and Jim had been too young to go to the war. They had gone to high school at Dillon, and, later to Bozeman, where they majored in farm management.

Neal had to tell them of being missing in Germany, of his stay at Letterman and the C.I.C. major who had been so good to him. Of Mrs. Beanor and Lee Simms and the old house, and Koma Kulshan he couldn't even see because of the huge snowbank. And, lastly, especially of Sister Marie Vincentia and Angela.

"I saw this thing happen in England after the first war," Dad Keith said. "We lost so many men some girls would do anything—anything at all—to marry, to leave, to live. We will do what Maria suggested. We will wait, but I doubt if Angela will return."

He put his arm on Neil's shoulder. "I hate to tell you this, but Cathy was so eager to see you first she tripped over a log and has a most splendid scab on one knee. You must be sure to write this to Mrs. Beanor. I am your third father and you are my eldest son, and thank God you have come home to us."

That night, in his room at the top of the house, Neal dreamed of Dad Westcott, clearly, distinctly, for the first time since his death. He thought they were all young again, in the old dining room, Maria serving the table, when suddenly Dad Westcott had raised his head and shot an arrow prayer up through the left corner of the ceiling thus:

"Your Honor, it is not my manner to complain, but, sir, it has been brought to my attention recently that here in the Cascades I have never seen the entire dome of heaven. It is true that if I lay on the very top of Koma Kulshan and gazed straight up, I would do fairly well. The trouble is, I would freeze before morning. If it is not impertinent, do you not agree this is inequitable?"

He woke up smiling, Tim III tucked in the curve of his back, purring softly.

"And if you think that when Cathy is up here with me, your head is going to be on the pillow between us, all I can say is that the time has come when a pussycat is going to find out he is a pussycat."

15. I Do, I Do

Cathy and Neal were married two weeks later in the garden. The children brought the wedding bouquet, made of wild flowers tied with ribbon. The mothers, who would not expect the bride to feed such an assemblage, brought potato salad, sandwiches, cookies, punch and the wedding cake. The minister drove twenty miles from Dillon. Pat Bennett, who had the only beauty parlor for miles around—a trailer off the road in the wilderness—arrived in time to see that Cathy's hair was worthy of her best talents, and contribute a marvelous molded salad. Keith-Hutton provided the ring, his mother's.

"It was my grandmother's also," he said. "I want it to stay in the family."

Because he absolutely refused to choose between them, both Ed and Jim were the best man. The girl Jim was going to marry was the maid of honor. Neal said "I do" twice. The meadow larks sat on the jack fence and sang all through the ceremony.

There were no elaborate wedding gifts. Only very simple things, but the men said shyly, "We've been giving some thought on what to give you and Neal, Cathy. If if pleases you, we've decided that when your dad buys the lumber for his barn, we'll all help him put it up."

The women said, "Now you two have a fine wedding trip and don't worry about a thing. We'll straighten up, put the dishes away and see that your menfolk don't starve to death."

Cathy and Neal drove to Helena for their honeymoon. At Butte they could see the lights shining on the famous old mines. It was dark when they reached the old Placer Hotel on Helena's main street, Last Chance Gulch, from which millions and millions of dollars of gold had been taken long ago. In the morning they strolled past the old brick building where Dad Westcott and Neal's father once had their offices. They looked at stone Victorian mansions. They found the house where Neal had lived with his father. Dad Westcott's house at Kenwood, then the suburbs, was gone in the new building. They saw the capitol, of course, with its copper dome, once so bare, now landscaped, and the historical museum with its Charles Russell paintings and statues. But the houses they liked best, that spoke to them, were the small old houses with their storm porches, painted, well kept, their yards colorful with flowers. They said, "We have lasted. We have endured because our ancestors cherished us."

"We'll come back again, and again," Neal promised. "I want to see the gates of the mountains."

The day they left Helena they had the hotel pack them a picnic dinner, and on the way home they turned up a small mountain road to eat it. Down through lush green grass came a flock of sheep. In the crimson sunset the grass turned suddenly wine-colored, and the white backs of the sheep seemed to flow down the mountain like a slow and gentle waterfall, beautiful beyond belief.

One day Cathy drove Neal to Twin Bridges where the Big Hole and the Beaverhead Rivers join to form the Jefferson. On the way they passed Beaverhead Rock which Sacajawea with Lewis and Clark had recognized as near her people, the Shoshoni. Another day they drove to see a pishkun, a bluff over which the Indians had driven the buffalo so the braves could kill them with bows and arrows, before they had acquired guns from the trappers and horses from the Spanish. And a third day, the smell of sage dry and warm, they drove to Nevada City and its twin mining camp, Virginia City, second capital of the territory, where gold had been discovered in 1863. Ten thousand people had lived once in Virginia City, which had been accurately and carefully restored.

They saw "Robber's Roost," a stage station, part bar, part dance hall, once frequented by fifty desperados calling themselves The Innocents, their leader a soft-spoken, charming psychopath, Harry Plummer, sheriff of Bannack, the first capital of the territory. The Innocents had mingled with the miners at the Roost and operated on the eighty miles of ravine and brushwood to waylay the stagecoaches and the miners with their take, killing a hundred and fifty and probably many more. Seeking advice from California, twenty-four Masons, many of them well-educated and destined for prominence in the making of the state, had formed the Vigilantes and wiped out Plummer's gang in three months.

Yet here the young people had gone on learning French, going on sleigh rides sponsored by the Literary Society and attending a performance of the opera *Griseldis*.

Cathy and Neal went to Boot Hill to look at the graves of the highwaymen and their old wooden markers. They climbed the steps of the museum, and Cathy showed Neal a picture of one of the early legislatures when Helena was made the capital. They looked long at Dad Westcott's picture, young, handsome and clean-shaven, surrounded entirely by a sea of whiskers. It had taken many years before the children had been born, and for the first time they realized he had been middle-aged when they could first remember him. They looked at the pictures of Colonel Wilbur Sanders, the brains of the Vigilantes.

"I remember," Neal said, "one time when we shared a tent in Butterfly Meadows Dad Westcott talked of Colonel Sanders whom he liked and admired. When the courts were established and the mob was going to hang a horse thief, Colonel Sanders stood on a wagon wheel and demanded the man be given a trial, and he was."

"In Dad's papers there is a letter from Sanders," Cathy said. "This was when the copper wars went on and on and on, with killings below ground. Helena was the capital then and fistfuls of money were tossed over the transoms of the old Placer hotel to buy votes and bribe judges. I remember Colonel Sanders wrote Dad that the great adventure was over in the battle of greed."

The past was so much a part of the present that they half expected to hear sounds from the old bars and laughter.

When they reached home the first load of lumber for the barn had arrived.

"Neal," said Keith. "I want you to return to Letterman and get your discharge. I have seen no sign of weakness in your ankle. You have put on ten pounds. No—Cathy can't go. We'll need her when the neighbors help put up the barn. But not one bit of hard work will I let you do until we are sure you are completely well."

Neal flew to San Francisco and checked in at Letterman. It was Major Miller who gave him the good news. He was completely well again. The money due him for the months he had been reported missing was ready for his signature. His ankle was well and strong.

"There's just one thing," the major said, smiling. "I hope you'll let me take you out to dinner. I promise not to eat much. I'll be too busy asking questions."

They had a sumptuous meal. Neal told him everything. Mrs. Beanor sending for Keith-Hutton. His return to the Cascades. His visit with Sister Marie Vincentia. He told him of old Nat and the sky that came down all around, of the marriage, of the past which was almost a part of the present. And especially of the people, the wonderful neighbors who had helped them always.

"Cathy and I want you to come visit us. I'll take you anywhere. Nat says he will fly you over the prairies in his gooney bird. Cathy says she will let you burp the baby, if and when we have one, we hope, we hope."

"I'll come. It's a promise. As a bachelor, I am a burper supreme."

He was silent, suddenly serious.

"You know, Neal, I wish our country had never picked up the pot of gold at the end of the rainbow. We are the most generous nation that ever existed, but history tells us that the nation that tries to straighten out the problems of the world starts out idealistically and nobly. It really believes that to be generous is to be liked and it's wrong. Other nations will ask its help, take all they can get, let it bind up their wounds. But the need to do so hurts their pride and they do not say thank you. And let the naive power blunder into some ancient feud, where it does not belong or even understand, and they will consider it stupid. I would like to think Americans will remember what Montana can tell us about the qualities that built this nation."

"And what were they?"

"Hard work, risk, trust and, above all, courage."

It was queer, but on the way home Neal had the strange feeling he had been talking to Dad Westcott.

When he returned, he went to work on the barn and when it was done, the family had a barn-warming and dance, two banjos and a guitar. It was a huge social success, the women keeping the coffee and food going, the men in little groups by themselves, discussing livestock prices. Every ranch wife knew well her husband might not remember to dance with her for at least two hours. Nat Burke was there with his son. They had found their ranch in the Madison Valley.

"Grain for me," Nat said, "and quarter horses for Thad. There is nothing more stimulating, as every Montanan knows, than sticking your neck out."

16. The Hard, the Free, the Lovely Years

These were the busy, the hard-working years that slip by so fast. Jim married and went to live in an ancient ranch house on the family property, long unused and in need of a general family overhauling.

Cathy and Neal produced three children, John, named for Dad Westcott, Keith, named for his grandfather, Keith-Hutton, and Kim, who, to Neal's delight, showed very early she resembled Cathy—she was a handful.

There was a time in the family—this was before it had acquired a dryer—when you could not enter the back door without getting smacked in the face with a frozen or wet diaper.

"Kim's wet again," Granddad Keith would say in tones of extreme martyrdom when the family was off on some outing. "Change her, Cathy, and when you return her to my lap be sure to put that bag of wet diapers in the back of the car. Even a doting granddad has to draw the line somewhere."

And Cathy would shoot up a quick and silent prayer, "Your Honor, please don't let them grow so fast. Let it last a little longer." His Honor said not a word.

The high chairs disappeared one by one. In no time at all even Kim was on the unabridged dictionary, and when dining out—a rare occasion—it was no longer necessary to push all the food to the other end of the table where she could not pick up something delightfully spillable and drop it on the floor with a gleeful chuckle.

"Every one of my grandchildren is going to be a 4-H member. I want each one to have some livestock of his choosing in recompense for the work he shares, sufficient to put him through college when the time comes."

For their help with the chores John and Keith were paid in heifers, each having his own brand for identification. Kim began with chickens.

"Wouldn't you know it?" said Granddad Keith-Hutton.

But Kim turned out to be a splendid den mother to her brood. She fed them. She watered them. They did superbly, that is, until one of the horses inadvertently stepped on one and broke her leg. Kim carried it, tears tumbling down her face, to Granddad Keith-Hutton, who put a splint on the leg. The chicken, splint and all, did well, except when Kim's flock decided to roost in a tree and she couldn't get up, and when they decided to rest in thick brush, and she couldn't get out.

Granddad Keith and Kim went to the store at Glen, and begged an empty cigar box. Then, with two sticks for dowels and four empty spools from Cathy's sewing box for axles,

Keith-Hutton made four small wheels and a tongue, and he harnessed the chicken to a small wagon. It ruined her. Kim named her Teezie and she became the snoot of the chicken yard. She was totally uninterested in roosters or eggs. Whenever the family went off on an errand, they were met upon return by several large friendly dogs of uncertain origin, Tim III, who dined on barn mice but always was hopeful that somebody would remember pussycats appreciate a saucer of milk, or at least a chance to lick the ice cream dish—and Teezie, safe forever from the skillet or the boiling pot.

When the family attended the small girl's May Day at the country school, all the little girls showing their pets bedecked with sunbonnets and paper posies, it was Kim, Teezie clucking happily along, pulling her little wagon, who won first prize.

"I'm too big for chickens," Kim announced solemnly. "I'm going in for sheep." And with her profits and additional assistance from Granddad Keith-Hutton she embarked with a ram and several ewes. When the lambs came there was always a bummer, a twin or triplet, and these Kim kept behind the kitchen stove, feeding them on a bottle until some ewes who had lost their lambs finally accepted them.

Kim had a pony now and rode with the family on the cattle drives. When the men and the boys were busy in the corrals at calving time and Neal was up all night in the barn with some eighty-five-pound calf whose mother refused to recognize it, he would call to the house for help: "Cathy, I'm frozen and I can't make this little bugger suck. Bring me a hot blanket and coffee." It was Kim who let Cathy sleep in sweet innocence and appeared in the night so cold the tears came to her eyes and froze on her lashes.

"Wrap the hot blanket around the calf," she'd say, like a wise old crone, and she would take the feeding bottle with the cow's milk and talk to the calf. "Come on, darling. Do it for Kim. Try the milk on my finger first." Kim had a way with every living thing that needed her, and Neal would think, "Dad Westcott must have felt for Cathy as I for Kim."

When branding day came, it was always done some distance from the house near some old corrals. The nearest neighbors appeared to help, as the family helped them. Custom demanded all males must be fed precisely at noon, a fact of ranch life all wives fortunately understood. And who was it who helped Cathy check the vaccine, the syringes, the disinfectants, the blood stoppers? It was Kim. Since every rancher was now his own cowhand, and some, like Neal, were not yet expert with the lasso, cotton was advisable for the ears, and when the calves were dragged bellowing from their mothers, the bulls castrated, the ears notched, the branding iron applied, who was it who went galloping to the house with a bucket of Rocky Mountain oysters which must be cleaned, dipped in batter, and deep fried? It was Kim, and if you don't know what a Rocky Mountain oyster is, don't ask.

Montana was not quite ready to face its complicated and difficult past. In its collective heart it knew it had made some of the mistakes the country had made. Too much, too soon! Too little, too late! But how it resented those smug eastern historians who insisted it had no men of true distinction. No artists except Charlie Russell, who was not exactly a Rembrandt. No great victories. No famous battlefields where huge armies had fought and died for liberty. It had trailed behind it a fairy tale, its cowhand a combination of Robin Hood and Sir Galahad, to the delight of Hollywood, which had turned him into a rip-snortin', hip-shootin' caricature and found romance in the heartbreak of the covered-wagon days.

On the capitol grounds was a statue of one Thomas Meagher, a warmonger of sorts, who had called out a volunteer militia—this had cost the government a million—for a war with the Sioux that never took place, Mr. Meagher, no doubt fortunately, disappearing in a dubious and mysterious death. It also had General Custer.

There is another peculiarity about Montana. Never, never, never ask friends and relatives to drop by "just any time," because they'll do it, usually unannounced and all at once. A well-trained ranch wife's reaction is instinctive and fast as an atom. She estimates the number of cars coming up the ranch road, swishes up the unmade bed, runs a comb through her hair, pops a huge roast in the oven, calls all offspring to start picking four gallons of string beans and five heads of lettuce, prays that the bakery wagon will arrive from Dillon so she won't have to bake, and opens the door, all smiles and affability. This art is nondeductible. No matter how good she gets, a ranch wife is not her husband's partner. The best she can hope to be is his survivor.

Cathy's first guests arrived this summer. There were a mere three—Lee Simms and his new bride—and Mrs. Beanor.

Neal was delighted to see Lee. Granddad Keith was his most charming to Mrs. Beanor, who was given, of course, the best bedroom and who announced that the one thing she wanted to see was the Custer National Monument. That night the children were sent to the barn to sleep in the hay so the grown-ups could settle down to a good talk. They did so. Almost immediately Kim called.

"Mother," said Kim. "Make Keith stop punching me in the nose."

"Punch him back," said Cathy firmly.

"But Mother, I did. It made his nose bleed."

"Badly?"

"Well-l, no. Just a little."

"If it doesn't stop, call me in five minutes." Silence!

With careful planning Mrs. Beanor was taken to the Custer National Monument. The day was overcast, the place lonely, ineffably sad.

"Which is the great man's grave?" asked Mrs. Beanor, and Neal showed her the stone which marked the place where he fell and replied gently that Custer was now buried at West Point.

It was now Kim's turn.

"Do you know what the older boys in my school say of Custer? They say he disobeyed orders, refused to wait for reinforcements and got himself and all two hundred and fifty of his men recklessly killed. They say anybody who thinks he was a great hero is a Custer nut."

Mrs. Beanor looked pained.

"Do you want to know what else they say? They say the Indians were our first pioneers. All they wanted was to be free, nomadic and pursue the buffalo. And what did we do to them? We shut them up on reservations and stole their lands and half starved them."

"Kim," said Neal firmly. "It wasn't quite as simple as all that. When the covered wagons arrived, the Civil War was over, the North broke, the South overrun with carpetbaggers and ruined. Roads were few and it was the Army's job to protect the covered wagons. The trouble was it couldn't keep them on the roads. They'd see a nice place to settle, right in the middle of an old Indian hunting ground, and get themselves massacred."

"And the boys in my class say that all the time the government was fussing around debating how to handle things, there was a man in Colorado who understood the Indians and said so, but nobody listened."

Mrs. Beanor looked as if she were about to faint.

"Now take Chief Joseph. All he was trying to do was to get his people safely to Canada without bloodshed. He outmarched, outfought and outsmarted the Army for eighteen hundred miles. With only three hundred warriors left and burdened with three hundred women and children, he surrendered at the Bear Paws. He had to, or see his people starve. That's where he made his famous speech, 'I will fight no more forever.'"

"Kim," said Neal slowly. "Unless you want us tossed out of our home state, subside."

Mrs. Beanor was given a lovely time. Neal and Lee Simms

shopped for a bull in Alberta so Mrs. Beanor could see Glacier National Park. It was Neal who put Mrs. Beanor on the train on the way to visit her Peter Rabbits.

"I am delighted with Cathy," she told him. "How glad I am I could be of such assistance to Judge Westcott. I just wish I were near enough to help you with that Kim. I shall think of you, dear, and pray. It's the only thing left."

Neal was inclined to agree. When the train had left, he shot up a fast one.

"Your Honor," said Neal, "if Kim must be punched in the nose, let it be by one of her brothers. Save her, please, from a Custer nut." His Honor answered immediately. The sky suddenly flashed with summer lightning. Great fat raindrops fell in the middle of a rainbow, each drop turned into a gloriously colored pearl.

The last night Lee Simms was there, he and Neal stayed up for a long talk.

"I was scared to death Kim would ask me what happened to Chief Joseph, 'the great eagle of the Wallowas.'"

"What did, Lee?"

"He died at Nespelen on the Colville Reservation in northern Washington. He died brokenhearted in a miserable little circle of teepees. Thirty miles away there is a dam bearing his name."

"How's Dad Westcott's tree, Lee?"

"Just the same. I don't think anybody has been up on that little glacier since he took you kids. There's not a week goes by someone doesn't speak of the Judge. But the town has grown very little. Life has passed it by. It's a beautiful place to retire."

When Lee left, Neal suffered a severe shock. His cute, sweet little Kim was no more. How long had this been going on, and why hadn't he seen it?

He took a leaf from the past, dropping into Kim's room for a bedtime chat. One night he spread out a map on her bed.

"We have seven Indian reservations, Kim, several of a million acres or close to it. In the thirties the Commissioner of Indian Affairs created a new Reorganization Act. The Act provided incorporation on a tribal basis. No land, power sites, water rights, oil, gas or mineral rights can be sold or mortgaged. The Flatheads incorporated first and are operating their own lands."

"Dad," said Kim slowly, "do you think Custer exceeded his orders recklessly?"

"Yes, I do."

"Does your conscience hurt when you think of Chief Joseph?"

"Yes, it does, Kim. But I also think Montana will have to take its own time facing the difficult past. That's hard and it hurts. And, by the way, I notice you have outgrown your pony. I am going to buy you a quarter horse. A mare, I think, so you can breed her later and have a colt to raise."

"Thank you."

"You know something, Kim. I have a funny feeling that the time will come when the Indians and the whites will have to fight together to keep the land and the life they love."

"Dad, will you tell me what part our families played in making this country, the way Granddad Westcott told you?"

"Yes, Kim, it's a promise."

Nat came to see them that week.

"Thad's been drafted for Vietnam," he said quietly. "I'm fine. I have my wheat to keep me busy. Keith-Hutton may need to help me with the horses."

"You'll have it, Nat. All the help you need. Whatever would I have done if you hadn't helped me until Ed and Jim were educated to take over."

17. Visitors

Montana, like the Cascades, touched the mind unforgettably. To Neal, who was accustomed to the sun rising slowly over the ranges, morning seemed to come at once like a daily miracle. He began the day looking over the corral across the barley fields, his heart thrilling to the beauty and the vastness. In the days when it was forty below, the sky gray-blue, his heart lifted to the shimmering frost crystals shining like tiny lights. And when a warm chinook began to blow softly, it was as if it spoke to him: "Fooled you. I was here all the time."

Neal knew every outcropping, every beaver pond, every mountain that always looked so much nearer than it was.

"I have come to know our land so well," he told Keith-Hutton, "that if you put me down anywhere upon it, surely my feet would find their way home sure as an eagle's wings. I know where the lodgepole wait on the middle range, and I know the quaken aspen that legend says quivered the day Christ was crucified and have never stopped. I know the cottonwoods when the cold comes slowly and they keep their leaves golden and beautiful, and I know the cattle coming down the slope, lowing, the steam from their nostrils blowing in the wind."

Keith-Hutton said, "I love those winter nights when clouds of snow come in spiral whirls, and all of us are at home with a book. Sometimes I can almost feel Dad Westcott's presence. I think he would be glad we are here and together. Life was not good to him, but he was good to life."

Each summer the 4-H'ers, as Keith-Hutton called them, sent a lad from some foreign land to learn American ways. One summer it was two Australians, queer-spoken, happy and outgoing, a joy to all. The second summer it was a young Scot who with his brother and mother owned a sheep farm near Edinburgh. He worked as hard as the boys and men. He ate anything. He washed his own clothes. He played the bagpipes and sent Tim running for the barn, and the dogs to cover their ears in the brush beneath the cottonwoods.

The third summer the family went to Idaho to a Basque festival.

The fourth summer the family had two most welcome and unexpected visitors. Major Miller arrived, soon to retire from service. The Orphanage of St. Joseph had its anniversary and the mother house at Newark sent Sister Marie Vincentia as its representative. The family visited her at once and suffered the same shock Neal had felt when he had first seen her. This was not her promised visit. This was a bonus, and since there was no nunnery near the ranch, she was permitted two days with the Westcotts.

The morning Neal brought her home it was upon a scene of utter devastation. Several coyotes, those sweet, harmless, doglike creatures who hurt nothing according to the wild-life fanatics, had attacked Kim's sheep. Four ewes stood, heads hung, the veins in their necks cut, slowly bleeding to death. They would have to be killed because a coyote's jaws and claws are foul with the putrefaction of his trade. On the ground lay five lambs, all in one piece except for the coyote's favorite tidbit, the liver.

Kim stood in tears, and when Sister Marie Vincentia saw Dad Westcott's granddaughter thus, she turned into Maria and took her in her arms to comfort her. Neal ran to the house to call Nat. But it was Thad who answered. He was home safe and sound after his four-year service.

"I'm in the army aircraft reserve," he said. "but I'm home safe. "I'll be right there. Load the rifles."

Thad set down the hedgehopper in the lower meadows.

"Hop in, Kim. Major, how are you as a shot?"

"Excellent."

"Sister Marie Vincentia, can you shoot a gun?"

"I was the best one on tin cans," said Maria modestly, "and not at all bad on skunks."

Major Miller took twine and tied it around Maria's chin and veil, knotting it firmly in the back so her hands would be free.

"It will be blowy and we'll have to keep the door open," Thad said. "Now, let me see. They can't be too far. They're probably sleeping off their fine meal under the trees higher up. We'll buzz them," and sure enough, six coyotes scrambled out from the sage and began to run for it.

Kim shot one, the major shot two. Sister Marie Vincentia shot three, her veils standing out straight behind her.

"Tomorrow we'll send one of the boys for the pelts. If I were you, Kim, I'd put a sign across the panel truck—EAT COYOTE LAMB AND DROP DEAD."

On Maria's last night they spoke almost entirely of the early summers in the Cascades.

"More than anything in this world I would like to see the little glacier that had no name," said Marie. "I know I can't. When my promised visit finally gets here, I might be able to ride a cayuse pack pony across Skyline Ridge, but I'll never, never be able to stand up when I get off."

When the family took Maria to the train it was almost as bad as the first time. There were tears in all the eyes except the major's.

"I spent the whole night writing a letter to the Mother Superior. On official stationery, of course. I thanked her for letting us have a brief visit. I said the Good Lord must have known we needed you, and that with your usual grace you had managed to help Dad Westcott's granddaughter through a traumatic experience for which we are all grateful."

"And if she questions me?" asked Maria very, very slowly.

"You will say you helped a young girl save the lambs that are going to put her through college. I have thought up a splendid line for you. 'After all, Mother, didn't Our Lord carry a little lamb in His arms?' That'll get her. Don't forget me, Maria."

"I wish I could."

The train began to move. Maria cried all the way through North Dakota. Then she was again her impeccable self.

The Mother Superior said to her, "I received the loveliest airmail letter from a Major Miller. What kind of a man is he?"

"He's a charming sinner."

"Sinners," said the Mother Superior quietly, "are our specialty. Now tell me about the orphanage."

18. Walk Gently This Good Earth

For the family these were still the growing years, close and loving. Cathy and Neal's oldest boy, John, was through college and had married a fine girl from Dillon. They were living in an old ranch house on the middle range near Jim and his wife, helping out with the family's herd while slowly building up their own. The second boy was in college, and Kim in high school at Dillon. The coyotes had not again attacked her sheep, which prospered. Her quarter horse had produced a colt. She had acquired from her father a most noble steer. In the summer she washed him carefully with the hose, brushed him, back-combed him into a sartorial splendor that brought her a neat profit at the county fair. She also had acquired her own brand. It was a chicken foot.

Butte was no longer the richest hill on earth. Now it was turning into a pit. The miners who had once fought terrible wars beneath the earth were teamsters, reduced in number, gouging low-grade ore in trucks with wheels twelve feet high, the shafts and drifts of the famous old mines, the Mountain Con, the Badger, the Emma exposed.

The roads in the big sky country were greatly improved and a pioneer Air Service had replaced the war buddies' hedgehoppers and gooney birds. Many a rancher owned his own Cessna to visit the Hereford show in Denver or seek a lost steer on his own range.

There was one dramatic change. Formerly the barley, oats, and alfalfa had been irrigated by flooding them from the stream that flowed down a ditch from the middle range. Now and slowly the family had acquired sprinkler pipes which must be moved twenty-three paces each morning and twenty-three paces each night. When the pipes were complete it was a sight to see, the crops green and beautiful in the falling water. Irrigation began in May when the northern lights turned the sky to radiance. Since the family's cattle arrived in the spring, they were sold at the weekly Butte auction in November. They were born in calving pens and wintered in the frozen meadows unless there was a bad storm. They were trailed to the middle range in April, and some two hundred to the high range in June.

When Kim entered college, majoring in farm management, she worked summers with the men. She was a whiz with a buck rake, spreading the grain which the men had cut with the swather, piling the grain ready to be stacked and fenced. The new sprinkling system did wonders for the crops, but it was expensive and kept the family in what Kim called "the financial fidgets."

It took the whole family to help move the sprinkling system, and the ranch came first. Major Miller had retired and asked Neal if he might rent and remodel an ancient house left over from some long-gone owner. He was a tremendous help and a born mechanic, working on the trucks, usually with Ed, who had not married because he was so badly needed at home.

One of the neighbors who helped them when it was their turn to get their cattle to the November auction had brought his cattle from California when he had come to join a widowed aunt and a cousin. His cattle calved in the fall and were sold in July. This took a huge communal effort. The neighbors assembled trailers and trucks and took eight loads to Butte to be sold the next day.

There are questions you do not ask a rancher: How many acres do you own? How much cattle do you buy or sell? It is like asking, "How much money do you have?" The auctioneer understood this and respected it. The next day when the auction was held, the seats filled with ranchers, many of them fine-looking older men whose eyes Lord Tweedsmuir had once called "the clear wise eyes of mountain men which are like no other." When the auctioneer reached the price agreed on for the neighbors' cattle he chanted, "Sold," and the cattle were whisked out. This time the old ranchers sat like stones. Totally quiet. They bought nothing. They sold ancient horses for dog meat, and worn-out cattle for hamburger. This had never before happened. The neighbors' cattle would be left a day or two and the communal cavalcade would bring them home and try again.

"I don't understand it," Ed told Keith-Hutton. "It was eerie."

"In the days of the copper wars one mining faction bought

up all the newspapers. If a rancher wanted to know what was going on in his own state he had to read out-of-state papers. He still does. He reads papers from New York, from California, from Denver. He follows closely the international comment in the best London editions."

"Then why are they waiting?"

"To see now that Nixon is president if he can get us out of Vietnam."

And sure enough. When after long negotiations Nixon announced the transfer of fighting to the South Vietnamese and the gradual withdrawal of our troops, the ranchers began to buy and the family took the neighbors' cattle back to the auction. This time they were sold.

Two months later Neal received a letter from the Mother Superior of Sister Marie Vincentia's order. She wrote, "I think the time has come for Sister Marie Vincentia's promised visit. I think she should come by air and we will pay her fare. She is frail and the doctor says no trip must be too strenuous. She talks of little else but the early happy summers. I know I can trust your discretion."

Cathy was appalled. "Oh Neal, how can the years have slipped by so fast? How can we have her now? But we must. It's obviously urgent."

"Leave it to your adopted dad," Keith-Hutton said. "The major and I will call Lee Simms and see if he has any suggestions."

Lee did indeed. "There's a new road that takes off at Burlington, north of Seattle. It goes across the North Cascades in the eastern part of the Koma Kulshan National Forest which Maria has never seen. From there it goes into the new North Cascades Park. It is going to be one of the marvels of our country. It is not done yet, but we can drive Maria slowly and easily to the part that is completed, where the new Paysaten wilderness will begin. It is designed for youth. No roads or vehicles permitted. Hikers and pack trips and mountain climbing yes, but even the mosses and wild flowers are to be protected. We'll take my car and I will meet you and Maria in Seattle. I promise it won't be too strenuous and it is unforgettable."

"It's all arranged," Keith-Hutton told Cathy. "You and the major and Neal will fly to Seattle and meet Lee and Maria. The major and I are paying your fare and all accommodations. Lee is providing the car. I will stay home. The boys, Ed, Kim and I will look after the ranch. I will attend the 4-H demonstrations. I'll do everything but play the organ in church, and I'd do that if I knew how."

Lee met them in Seattle and Maria also. She had greatly aged. She seemed frail but happy. They drove to Burlington, where they stayed the night. By easy stages they drove to Marblemont and into the Ross Lake Recreational Center. They stopped at Newham. When they reached Diablo, they rode up the mountainside, car and all, on the automatic railroad which had carried all the construction material and machinery for the Ross Dam and the powerhouse for the Diablo Dam. No one ever forgot Maria's face when they reached the Diablo Lake overlook with its views of Thunder Creek to the hanging glaciers of Colonial and Pyramid peaks. Lee pointed out where the Paysaten wilderness would be.

"If I never see it again, I'll know it's safe for future generations," Maria said. "Do you remember when Dad

Westcott discovered Willa Cather and read *My Antonia* aloud to us? I remember she wrote that some memories were better than anything that could ever happen to you again. That's the way I felt about our summers, and this is like reliving the trips to the mountains Dad Westcott taught us to love."

They returned slowly. Keith-Hutton met them in Helena. While Maria was with them, it was the major who drove her to see Dad Westcott's picture in Nevada City, and when Cathy and Neal had an anniversary, it was Maria who insisted on cooking the dinner, her sleeves rolled up and pinned. She cooked all the dishes they remembered and loved. She not only cooked them, she insisted on serving as she had always done, over Cathy's protests.

"I suppose I'll have to sell a bull and give you a ruby, my love," Neal said to Cathy.

"I'd rather have a new separator."

"Good. You can get me a pair of boots with hard toes. A struggling calf always seems to land on my toes."

When they put Maria on the plane to fly east, there were no tears. She hugged them and kissed them, her face still radiant.

Several months later the Mother Superior wrote of her death from a rare anemia. She had died in her sleep.

"She told me to tell Major Miller she had adopted him as one of the family, and loved him, too. She even told me about the coyotes. She said she never would have come to us knowing anything about love, how to give or receive it, if it hadn't been for her Westcotts. We are grateful to you. May God bless and keep you."

Cathy answered it and put the letter with Dad's sonnet. When the family had one of its mechanical days, the pump obstinate and everyone away from the house, she cried.

"I'm a heartbreaker," she thought, "but it's always my own heart I break. Oh, Maria, I was so small when my mother died of heart trouble, I can scarcely remember her face. The twins can't remember her at all. You took her place. Did I ever thank you?"

Maria's summer, they called it. "Do you remember the look on her face when she saw the Diablo viewpoint?"

Maria's summer.

19. *Am I the Last?*

President Thieu strenuously objected to doing his own fighting, and the Congress forbade Nixon to take on any more commitments without its approval. The withdrawals continued slowly, but when it was known Nixon had sent troops into Cambodia and Laos, student demonstrations were widespread and resulted in the killings at Kent State.

It was then Thad was called back into action, and he came at once to see Major Miller and Neal.

"It means an end to 'search and destroy,' to fire zones and armed helicopters. Nixon's going to use B-52 bombers to get us out. There's just one thing that worries me."

"I know what it is," Neal said quickly. "Your father. Old age needs to be to the respected, loved and needed. We'll bring him here."

"He can live with me," Major Miller said. "That's no problem, Thad. If you don't get back, we'll look after him."

"What do you mean 'if Thad doesn't get back'? Of course he'll get back!" It was Kim not yet returned to college from Christmas holiday. She had come in quietly and she was mad. "He has to get back because ever since he and Maria and the major and I shot the coyotes who were killing my sheep, I have considered him mine and I intend to marry him."

There was an appalling silence.

Thad took her hands. "Kim," he said, "If I were younger there's nothing in the world I'd rather do than toss you over my saddle and ride into the sunset. I'm too old for you."

"Oh, no, you're not! I don't want a dissenter. I don't want one of those hippies we've seen in Canada. If you're scared to ask me, I'll ask you. I'll chase you all over the meadow with the hay rake and mow you down, and don't think I won't." And out she went, slamming the door behind her.

"There are times," said Neal slowly, "when a parent doesn't understand his children at all. I am beginning to think she's smarter than we are, and I admit I feel much better."

"In all, we've had almost five hundred twenty-five thousand men in Vietnam," said Major Miller. "Now, Thad, I don't know where the B-52 bombers will be based. Thailand maybe, landing in Guam. If you get hit over the Hanoi-Haiphong area, if you can help it, don't be taken a prisoner. When it's over, a few POWs will be returned. We'll probably never know what happened to many of our men."

"I've thought of that. If I can, I'll use one of their tricks. Keep the enemy from being able to tell a friend from the foe. I'll ditch my clothes, darken my face and mingle with the noncombatants. And major, tell Kim to call my father Granddad. He's always wanted a granddaughter."

"I will. When you surface, give my name. I think we're crazy. I'm almost sure of it, but I must say I like it."

Nixon responded to the raids across the DMZ by ordering the mining of ports and heavy bombing of the Hanoi-Haiphong area. The last troops were withdrawn, and representatives of North and South Vietnam signed peace pacts in Paris. At the end, 1,560 POWs came home, and they came off the planes gallantly, like men. Thad was not among them. Major Miller and Neal helped old Nat to lease their ranch, and they brought him to the major's home.

Mr. Nixon made his triumphant trip to China. It cannot be said he won the Vietnam debacle, but he ended it, which was more than the Democrats, who had started it, could do. The whole country brightened considerably. Hope lifted her lovely head, and Kim managed to sneak home from college at every possible opportunity and tuck Granddad Burke in her pocket.

To Neal there was something very touching about her devotion to him, and his to her. If a horse jumped a fence and got himself lost on a neighbor's property, Kim, Granddad Burke beside her in the pickup, would be off on the search, laughing and talking with a joy that flabbergasted Cathy.

"When they're little, they step on your toes," she said dramatically. "When they're older, they step on your heart. Oh, Neal, she has that poor old man so bedazzled, it's scarcely decent to watch. My innocent little Kim! What'll we do? If Thad doesn't come back, his father will probably shoot himself, and Kim will marry some outlandish dissenter

with whiskers tied back in ribbons and take to the open
road."

"I think not," Neal told her. "After all, she's your daughter. I do not know how we survived some of your tomboy
escapades. But look at what domesticity has done for you,
my love. It has turned you into a lady—well, almost, anyway.
We shall continue to be optimistic."

"Your Honor," said Cathy furiously, "keep me from
punching him in the nose."

When Mr. Nixon returned from China and fell in disgrace
at Watergate, Neal called together all Maria's Westcotts, old,
new and adopted. They met in the main ranch house, and
they looked as glum as the clams Dad Westcott had found on
Chowder Ridge.

"It is obvious," said Neal, "our age of innocence is over.
The trouble with us is we can't say no. While we were
spending sixty billion rebuilding Europe, we neglected our
own problems. In fact, we made hash out of them. We are
young. We are naive. We've been taken and nobody likes us.
I don't want any one of us to come down with the shakes
and shivers. We're in for some hard times, and something
tells me they'll get a lot worse before they get better. The
Democrats will undoubtedly put Nixon where he'll have to
resign or be impeached."

"May I speak?" asked Granddad Burke.

"You may."

"Then let me point out we are the only nation on earth
strong enough to oust a president without a civil war or a
revolution."

Cathy forgot herself. "Nixon deserves it," she admitted,

"but wasn't it Ted Kennedy who walked away from Chappaquiddick with a two-month suspended sentence?"

"Cathy, my dear, will you please go to the kitchen and make us a large pot of coffee. You may leave the door ajar."

Cathy went to the kitchen. Oh, how she longed for Maria to comfort her. "Your Honor," she said, "he's impossible. He's imperious. Keep me from kicking him in the shins."

"We have one serious problem. It's those old ranchers. Any day now they will send me clippings from the London weekly or the God knows what. They'll raise the hair off our heads. What's more, I'll have to read them because they'll question me. Have I any volunteers?"

Granddad Burke stood up. "They can't raise my hair. I haven't any. I don't want to brag, but I know less about more things than any man alive. I'll answer them. I'll give you a careful, painless report."

"Bless you, Granddad."

If the family managed to keep its equanimity while all about them were losing theirs, it was due in large part to Granddad Burke.

It was always pleasant to see some wise old rancher approach with a twinkle in his eyes.

"Neal," he would say, "I can't tell you how much I enjoyed that letter Granddad Burke said you asked him to write about charisma. How I abominate that word! As you said, Hopkins invented a sure way to elect anybody with charisma for any office whatsoever. He did it for FDR and I must say, it worked. Promise the people anything and spend, spend on them. Tax it back, but do it cleverly. Elect, elect, elect. You know, I hated Nixon so much I would have enjoyed confronting him with a hayfork. He had been licked for the presidency. He had been licked as governor of his own state. He had no charisma. Not an iota. Pat did, but he didn't. Even the press didn't like him. When he got power, it went to his head and he forgot—now let me see, it was Sophocles, wasn't it, who said that a nation with great power is cursed. It starts out to be noble and ends up evil. Darn if I'm not a little sorry for the man."

Or this: "Neal, I cherish that letter Granddad Burke said you asked him to write in answer to that blast from the ex-President of Mexico, who announced it was our duty to take on the problem of the seventy-three percent of Africans, the forty-six percent of Asians and the twenty-seven percent of Latin Americans who do not know the alphabet. I wrote him that we were no longer a huge empty country with unlimited room. I wrote that we could not feed the world, but that we could help the needy of the world to help themselves."

"Neal," said Cathy, "you are milking that poor old man's brains."

"I am indeed. It keeps him busy and it keeps us from falling apart at the gussets, especially you, my pet."

Three days later Cathy and Neal went to Dillon and had their first encounter with an event occurring all over the country. They were approached by three solemn crows, Old Testament open, the Book of Revelation in hand.

"Repent and be saved," they begged. "The old prophecies are about to be fulfilled. You can read them right here. The Messiah is going to lift us to a better world any moment now."

"And the rest?" asked Cathy meekly.

"The rest will perish at Armageddon."

"Thank you," said Cathy. "It is awfully nice of you to ask us. Our neighbors to the south are Baptists. To the west they're Catholics. To the north they are Lutherans. As for me, I play the organ in the Presbyterian Church. I'm not much good, but I show up. All our neighbors have helped us, as we have them. I will have to decline. I'll take my chances at Armageddon with those we love."

The old crows shook their heads sadly and passed on.

"Granddad Burke couldn't have said it better. I have underestimated you."

"It must be catching. I'm ashamed to say I enjoyed it."

Soon after Nixon's resignation and Kim was through college, something very strange happened. The Forest Service sent down word that the cabin the family always used on the high range had been vandalized. Furthermore, some strange cult was slaughtering cattle, mutilating the sexual parts, draining the blood and departing without a sign, and rustlers with trucks and ramps were stealing cattle right off the ranges. For the first time it was necessary to take out insurance, and never, never to leave the house unlocked or the ranch unguarded. When Ed and Keith-Hutton caught two rustlers stealing cattle from the lower range and could identify them, they so testified at their trial. The rustlers were given a stiff sentence and fine. Both were suspended. When they returned to report to Major Miller and Granddad, the major's house was empty.

"Thad's surfaced," said Keith-Hutton. "Your Honor, bring him back in one piece."

The family waited, and they waited, and they waited. Poor Kim was totally repentant.

"It's all my fault," she wailed. "I even said I'd mow him down with the hay rake. And you, Mother, always such a lady."

One night after a time that had seemed interminable, someone noticed lights in the major's house. Nobody dared go over for fear Thad would turn up minus a leg or two. They prayed for courage that wouldn't come. Presently footsteps approached the door.

"You go, Ed," begged Neal.

"No, you go, Jim."

Keith-Hutton opened the door. There they stood, the three of them, looking well pleased with themselves, if not downright smug. Thad, appearing to be in one piece, was brown as a nut.

"Don't stand there!" cried Neal. "Say something! Where have you been?"

"Walking," said Thad. "Putting one foot in front of the other. I made the first run from Thailand across the Hanoi-Haiphong area to Guam. On our second strike the plane was hit. It wobbled. Pieces fell off. We managed to keep it flying until we were far past the danger zone, and night was falling. Then we bailed out, hid our parachutes, and discussed what to do. We knew it wasn't safe for all of us to stay together. Most of the crew planned to disappear among the South Vietnamese noncombatants. The navigator and I decided to walk to Thailand. This shows how love addles the brains. I was sure it was a mere matter of three hundred miles. Now I think it was closer to five hundred. Some missionaries who were hiding out took us in, tanned us with some local concoction, burned our clothes and found clothes for us to wear. We got along fairly well. The South Vietnamese were fleeing also with what they could carry, and we helped them, and they helped us. We got lost. We had dysentery. We had to hole up to heal our feet. Finally we reached U-Tapao. It's an American military airport south of Bangkok. The Army flew us back with a planeload of refugees from Cambodia and Laos. When I reached the base where I was drafted, Dad and Major Miller were waiting. The hospital gave me some shots, fattened me, and called a doctor to heal my feet. I'm fit, but I'm advised to take no huge walks for three months. Kim, stop blubbering like a scared rabbit."

"But, Thad, I was so outrageous."

"What do you think kept me going all that time?" And he held out his arms and she crept in, and suddenly everyone in the family was laughing and talking, tears streaming down their cheeks.

They were married in the home ranch house.

"I will stand for the ceremony," announced Thad, "but the altar will have to come to me." It did. Kim and Thad sat on the sofa to receive all well-wishers. The beloved neighbors were there, of course. The gifts ran mostly to soft doeskin Indian moccasins, huge carpet slippers, and one pair of handknitted baby booties, size eleven, ornamented with posies and ruffles. The neighbors said it was the most hilarious wedding they had ever attended.

Thad had discussed his and old Nat's ranch with Neal. "You need Kim as much as I do. For our honeymoon Kim and I are going to drive around a bit. She'll do the driving and I'll sit and look and look and look. Dad's and my ranch is leased to a friend who wants to buy it. In these times I think it might be well to keep it in the family. Dad has invested his money. I'd like to bring a few of my best horses here if I may. With what I have coming from the Air Force, Kim and I can build ourselves a little house and I can help Ed and the boys."

"You can use the guest bedroom in the ranch house, Thad. There's plenty of room for your horses. Let's let your ranch ride for a time."

In the joy of Thad's homecoming and the hubbub of conventions, primaries and the coming election, Montana was never quite sure just when President Ford announced the North Central Renewal Study which declared we must be free of reliance on imported fuel by 1985.

For the first time a twinge of real fear ran through the ranchers, even the wise old ones. They gathered in little groups and discussed it up and down.

There were in Montana millions of tons of low-grade coal, thirty percent of it on the Crow and Cheyenne reservations. It lay forty feet beneath the surface. To strip-mine it meant to enclose the acreage in a high steel fence and explode the yellow-brown earth. The dragline stood 215 feet high, requiring a generating plant of 200,000 megawatts to make electricity. A coal gasification plant required a million acre-feet of water to be converted into steam and lost. It was promised the land would be recovered and replanted, but the first tests were extremely dubious. It meant mobile homes for the workers, noise, ugliness, confusion.

The coal companies moved in. An occasional rancher who had coal on his land and could not resist a check for $125,000 or more sold his coal, found his neighbors no longer friendly. But most ranchers refused. "The land renews itself and continues to produce food. We will never sell. We love our life and will not give it up." The Crows, a happy, friendly people, leased a huge acreage, then asked the Department of Interior to cancel the contract, hoping for more money. The Cheyenne, a fierce, aloof, moralistic tribe, also leased a huge acreage, but when they understood just what it meant, hired an attorney and asked the Department of Interior to cancel the contract. Montana's leading historian called it what it was, a rape of the plains.

One day Neal and Thad met at Dillon an old Cheyenne chief to whom Granddad Burke had delivered medical supplies in his gooney bird days, and who remembered him. The chief said, "I did not go to school. My sons go. You and I fight now on the same side."

Another time when Cathy and Neal went north on business, they heard a terrific blast and saw a huge explosion of dirt fill the sky. Some rancher was selling out. "Here comes Armageddon," Cathy said. "Any minute now."

Thus Montana, Republicans and Democrats and Indians, fought the old, old enemy, greed.

"It isn't fair," Neal said. "We want to do our part. In thirty years American skill will have come up with new sources of fuel. But by that time we will have lost what we hold most dear."

Cathy worked harder than anybody. She was on the County Planning Board, which raised its own money and made recommendations to the legislature. The major, Keith-

Hutton and Granddad Burke helped present them, well-spoken and so well-informed they were successful in putting through needed zoning restrictions. Cathy worked for the 4-H'ers and was secretary for the county Republicans. The whole family went twice to Helena and succeeded in stopping a proposed dam across the Ruby which would have inundated a whole valley, including their lower ranch.

It was Neal who grieved most for his state and for his country. America had fulfilled its dream. It had molded people who had come here because they could not bear their lives, who had gone through all manner of hardship to turn out a multitalented American, a man like no other. Were we too going to end up a socialized state where a man could no longer make a living in his own way in his own time?

He sought to reconcile the heartaches of his generation with the present, and found solace in strange places. On an old Indian trail where the marks of the travois still showed. The smell of sage after rain. Going home at night to the family still close, still loving. The meadowlarks. The nighthawks, white dots on their underwings. On the high ridge, the gnarled tree, its heartwood still sound. And above all else, in space to lift the soul and make it grow.

The pit at Butte was huge now. Neal was always impressed by the old miner out of work and having a very hard time. His house was always in repair, the grass cut and trimmed. He might be in desperate need of welfare but never, never would he take it, sustained by the old pride, his smile always first, quick and friendly.

Neal was touched also by some of the old mansions of Helena, so unlike what many people would expect. Built of stone, built to last, showing a Victorian, a Queen Anne, an Italianate influence. The great of the world had been entertained in them. He looked a long time at the Wilbur Sanders home. He knew both Dad Westcott and his father had been asked to this house many times.

"You know, Thad," Neal told him one day. "Now that Carter is president and the country waiting to see what he'll do, there's one thing I dread."

"I know. It's Kim, Dad, and the major, Ed, Keith-Hutton and I have talked it over. My Kim is like Cathy. She collides with life. One of these days she's going to land on us like a young inquisitor. Let's talk to her. Get Cathy to ask us all to dinner on some cold Sunday night."

"That's easy. She was suggesting it the other day."

It was raining the night the family met, everyone present, no emergencies of any kind, for a miracle, the dinner excellent, as were all Cathy's dinners.

"You know, Neal," Thad said, "I notice the travelers who come to Montana this year are different."

"That's right," Dad Burke said. "They're like the animals of Africa driven south by years of drought, who return to their home valleys and mountains. Americans are like that. They are seeking their own roots, especially the young."

"It's the young I worry about. Youth looks ahead. It has only one dimension. But this is not enough. A man lives ahead, but unless he balances it with what his father, his great-grandfathers learned, what he knows is of little value."

Now it was Kim's turn.

"Dad," she said, "what do you think your generation has accomplished?"

"Well, dear, you don't have to see a friend crawl around the floor like a worm because he had polio and will never walk again. I did. Those faces terribly pitted with smallpox are gone now. Pneumonia doesn't kill people in five days. Nor typhus. Nor cholera. TB is practically gone. Also your life expectancy has increased forty years. You're not all bones as we were. The cold weather gives you a huge appetite. Of course, your feet are bigger."

"Child labor is gone," Ed said. "You don't have to wait until you are forty to marry because of a depression and you have parents to help. You've seen us begin to fight pollution and for conservation, both more difficult than we ever imagined. We haven't licked cancer yet, but we're coming closer and we will. I hate to admit this, but we're still stuck with the common cold."

"We've tackled racial prejudice," Major Miller said. "It's true, we were slow, but we almost tore our country apart to end slavery and save the Union. The black Americans fought long and bravely. We have not licked prejudice entirely. But we've licked ninety percent of it, and our older black Americans know it."

"Women can work at fair wages and their equality continues to grow," said Cathy.

"Dad, do you think we are horribly materialistic?"

"I think our huge middle class is the most generous group in the world. It knows affluence without simplicity is useless."

"Granddad Burke, will President Carter make mistakes?"

"He will. We're terribly new at international diplomacy.

But I notice most people in the world want to stay alive. I don't belive you could make an American drafted army engage in a holocaust in Africa."

"Then you don't think an atom war is possible?"

"Yes, I think it's possible. It only takes one maniac to start a war. Look at Hitler. Of one thing I'm confident. There will be no last American. A man who has known freedom is not going to give it up. There will always be weaklings who find it easier to live on welfare than work for a living. There will always be young men who will live on unemployment insurance while they ski in winter or practice putting in Florida. There will always be do-gooders who think we should take care of anyone in need, even if we end in the poor house. We cannot feed the world. We can help it help itself. Above all else, we cannot step into those danger spots where our interests are small, where old resentments have been festering since before we were colonies."

"Dad," Kim said very slowly. "Would you want to live your life over again?"

"Kim, no man has that choice. If he wants to live his life over, it is usually because he had a life so trivial, it cannot be said he lived at all. I am confident of one thing. If Democrats, Republicans, union leaders and all the rest of us will remember we are Americans first, nobody can defeat us. I'm sorriest for youth. It needs a natural hazard to help it grow into maturity. If it's given too much, it creates dangerous hazards of its own. We have seen the wonder and known the beauty of a new land. We have given years of our lives in depression and war which demanded what Dad Westcott called 'courage with grace.' We have known the joys of close families, the wonders of love and the agony of losing it, and this, Kim—this—"

Kneeling at his feet and holding his hands tight, she said, "Ssssh, I know what it is, darling. You've shown me. You've all shown me. This is to know the singing sadness man calls life."